DEAD DRUNK

Longarm eased his gun out of his holster. The table blocked it from view and he cocked the weapon, hoping he was still sober enough to shoot straight.

Lance turned his gun on Della. "You're a whore who deserves to die!"

"Marshal," Dudley hissed. "Do something!"

Longarm took a deep breath. He was seeing things in double vision so he closed one eye and shouted, "Mister, drop your gun!"

Lance swung his aim at Longarm. "You must either be dead drunk or real stupid! I'm the one holding the gun and you're doing nothin' but flappin' your gums. I hate marshals and I have just decided to kill all three of you!"

Longarm knew the man was serious and so he yanked up his gun and fired. His first slug missed Lance and drilled a picture of a naked lady hanging on the wall. Drilled her right between the eyes. But his second shot was on target and it caught Lance about two inches below his throat, knocking him out the door and into the street.

Della let out a cry and fainted.

Dudley's hand was shaking as he reached for the bottle of whiskey. "Marshal, you sure did kill that man."

"Well," Longarm said, "he sure did need killing."

Longarm and Dudley staggered out the door and paused to study Lance and the crowd that had gathered around his body.

"Better pass the hat," Longarm said, fumbling in his pockets and finding two silver dollars which he threw down between the dead man's feet. "Even a jealous fool deserves a decent burial . . ."

TABOR EVANS

LONGARM

AND THE NEVADA SLASHER

JOVE BOOKS, NEW YORK

LONGARM AND THE NEVADA SLASHER

A Jove Book / published by arrangement with
the author

PRINTING HISTORY
Jove edition / March 2001

All rights reserved.
Copyright © 2001 by Penguin Putnam Inc.
This book, or parts thereof, may not be reproduced in any form
without permission.
For information address: The Berkley Publishing Group,
a division of Penguin Putnam Inc.,
375 Hudson Street, New York, New York 10014.

The Penguin Putnam Inc. World Wide Web site address is
http://www.penguinputnam.com

ISBN: 0-515-13030-3

A JOVE BOOK®
Jove Books are published by The Berkley Publishing Group,
a division of Penguin Putnam Inc.,
375 Hudson Street, New York, New York 10014.
JOVE and the "J" design
are trademarks belonging to Penguin Putnam Inc.

PRINTED IN THE UNITED STATES OF AMERICA

10 9 8 7 6 5 4 3 2 1

Chapter 1

United States Deputy Marshal Custis Long stepped into Marshal Billy Vail's spartan office and eased into a chair. Placing his boots up on Billy's scarred and cluttered desk, he smiled and said, "The boys tell me that you have a tough assignment for me in Nevada."

"Word gets around fast," Billy said, frowning at Longarm's boots. "Do you mind taking your feet off my damned desk?"

Custis removed his boots and plucked a cheap cheroot from his vest pocket. He offered it to his boss with a smile. "Have a smoke?"

"I would rather smoke rope than your cheap, smelly cigars. Good heavens, man, why don't you buy some decent Cubans? Or at least something from the South. Those Mexican cigars will kill you one of these days."

Longarm struck a match against his holster and inhaled, then blew a smoke ring that spun lazily over Billy's round and slightly balding head. "If this job ever started paying me enough to buy good booze and good tobacco, I might consider it. But until then, I'll just take my humble pleasures where I can."

"I expect you will," Billy agreed. "It will always be wine, women, and song for you."

Longarm feigned indignation. "Aw, there's nothing wrong with the way I live. And you know you can count on me for the worst damn jobs this federal agency has to offer. So what kind of a miserable assignment do you have waiting for me in Nevada?"

Billy shuffled some papers. He made a sharp physical contrast to Longarm who stood six-foot-four in his stockings and had the shoulders of a lumberjack. In comparison, Billy was short, dumpy, and well aware that he was aging fast. Once, he'd been a marshal like Longarm, but the pressures of raising a family had dictated that he take a promotion and ride a chair instead of a horse. It was a change that he'd often regretted, especially when one of his deputy marshals came back from a tough but exciting field assignment.

"Well?" Longarm asked.

"I'm not sure what to make of this Nevada trouble," Billy admitted. "It involves murder and robbery."

"Doesn't sound too complicated. They go hand in hand."

"Yeah, I know that," Billy said. "But these Nevada murders don't seem to have any pattern or purpose."

Longarm shrugged. "Robbery needs no other purpose than to fill a criminal's pockets. What's really bothering you?"

Billy leaned back in his chair and drew a corncob pipe from his vest pocket. "We've been friends for a long time, haven't we?"

"Sure. You've always been fair."

"Then I have to tell you that this assignment is probably going to be more difficult and dangerous than anything you've handled in the past."

"Why so?"

2

"First off," Billy said, "our director has assigned you a partner."

Longarm stiffened. "You know I work alone."

"I know and so does the director. But he has this friend who has a son that we hired in Boston and—"

"Boston!" Longarm snorted. "Billy, you're not going to pair me off with some fool kid from the East, are you?"

"I have no choice. Maybe he won't be so bad."

"And maybe he'll get me killed!" Longarm said hotly. He came out of his chair and began to pace up and down. "I don't get it. First you tell me that this job is going to be extremely dangerous . . . and in the next breath you want to harness me to some greenhorn kid from Boston. You know that doesn't make sense."

"I know it, but the director must owe this friend a big, big favor. Either that, or the guy has some clout with the feds in Washington, D.C. But whatever the reason, my hands are tied."

Longarm returned to his chair. "Fill me in on what you know about the job . . . then the kid."

"I don't know much," Billy admitted. "For about the last year, we've heard rumors that someone was randomly murdering people in and around Reno, Carson City, and the Comstock Lode."

"That's a lot of territory."

"I know. I know. It seems that the murders always take place at isolated locations. One time a farm, another a mining claim, then maybe a ranch. This last one involved the murder of two men who were cutting timber on the eastern slope of the Sierras. Someone just came into their logging camp and shot them dead."

"You said something about robbery."

"Yeah," Billy agreed, "I did. Robbery does seem to be the motive for the killings. In every instance, money and valuables were taken. But, on the other hand, the people who have died were not wealthy."

3

"Maybe," Longarm said, "they were but only the killer or killers realized the fact."

"That's possible."

"What about the local authorities?"

"The marshal and his deputy in Reno are taking the murders very seriously but they don't have the manpower to go out and spend a lot of time in the country where they are taking place. The marshal there feels that his main responsibility is to the people who got him elected . . . the folks in Reno."

"I can understand that." Longarm scowled. "What about the authorities in Carson City and Virginia City?"

"They feel the same way despite the fact that people are getting pretty nervous and upset."

Longarm blew another smoke ring over Billy's head. "Why are we feds being called in? Sounds like a local problem to me."

"The last man to die was carrying United States mail. He was a courier and the mail he carried was missing when they found his body two weeks after he had disappeared. He was shot near a place called Franktown."

"I know where that is," Longarm said. "Has anyone seen the murderer or have we gotten at least some clue as to his identity?"

"Nope."

Longarm found that hard to believe. Almost all murderers left *some* evidence—footprints, hoofprints, spent cartridges, and other details that a good lawman would observe and note. "How many murders have there been already?"

"We can't be sure," Billy admitted. "With a killer who strikes one place and then the next without any pattern, you just can't say for sure. There have been at least twenty-five unsolved murders in those areas. Who knows how many were committed by the same person or persons? I'm afraid we've little to go on at the start."

"You've *nothing* to go on," Longarm corrected.

"That's why we need you," Billy told him. "I told our director that you're the only one who could solve the case."

Longarm scoffed. "And in response, he saddled me with a greenhorn. Billy, didn't you tell him that an inexperienced man could get us *both* killed?"

"Yeah, I tried to tell him that."

"And?"

"As you know," Billy said, "he likes to talk a lot better than listen."

"What if I refuse this assignment?"

"Then we are both in the doghouse. I was hoping for a promotion, but that would go out the window."

Longarm shook his head. "You're putting me between a rock and a hard place."

"Then just turn it down," Billy suggested. "I'll ask Mack Wilson."

Longarm groaned. "Mack would kill a greenhorn partner for certain. And he isn't one to show patience. You know as well as I do that he'd probably just mess everything up."

"I know." Billy raised his hands, palm upward in a gesture of futility. "But what choice would I have if you refuse?"

"What's the Boston kid's name?"

"Dudley. Dudley L. Applewhite. But the director says he prefers to be called 'Lucky.' "

"Oh for crying out loud!" Longarm scoffed with derision. "If he comes with me, I'll call him Dud . . . or worse. You met him?"

"Nope."

"How long has he been in law enforcement?"

"I don't know, but it can't be very long given his age."

"And that would be?"

"Lucky is eighteen."

5

" 'Eighteen!' " Longarm wailed. "The kid is still wet behind the ears. He might even be wearing diapers!"

"Calm down now," Billy said. "The director tells me that Lucky stands well over six feet tall and is quite a handsome lad. Says that he is plenty capable of taking care of himself under bad circumstances."

"I'll just bet," Longarm groused. "Can he handle a gun?"

"I have no idea."

"When can I meet Dud?"

"He'll be arriving from Boston tomorrow. The director expects you both to be on the train to Reno the very next morning." Billy filled his corncob pipe, avoiding Longarm's hard glare. "Why don't you at least agree to meet the kid before you turn this assignment down flat? Could be the kid is better than we imagine."

"If he's really from Boston, I find that difficult to imagine."

"He's a federal deputy marshal," Billy said. "He had to have something on the ball or he wouldn't have gotten hired . . . even in Boston."

"Naw," Longarm argued. "He got hired because he has connections. I'll bet Dud is a paper pusher. He's probably white as snow and weak as a kitten. Probably doesn't even shave yet and can't stand up to a hard wind."

"Meet him and then make up your mind," Billy urged. "At least give it that much."

"Why should I?"

"How about for our careers? Or at least mine, if you don't care about your own."

"All right," Longarm reluctantly agreed. "But I'm taking the rest of today and tomorrow morning off. I'll meet Dud this time tomorrow in your office. With any luck at all, he probably lost his nerve and never left the Boston train depot."

Billy grinned. "That would solve our problem, all right.

In the meantime, I have a file related to some of the unsolved Nevada murders. You might want to look it over."

"No, thanks," Longarm replied going to the door. "If I have to pair up with Dud, I'll read the file on the way west. If I refuse and get fired, then I won't have wasted my time."

Billy stood up. "Custis, what you have to keep firmly in mind is that people are being murdered in Nevada. Murdered randomly and wantonly. And while I understand why you'd be upset about being forced to take a greenhorn as a partner, the fact of the matter is that whoever is killing and robbing those folks needs to be brought to justice."

Billy tapped the file. "If you read this, you'd see that some of the killings have been brutal and gruesome. Not just bullets, but knives have been used to cut throats. In some cases, it appears that the murderers have tortured their victims before killing them."

"Probably to get them to tell where their money was hidden," Longarm said.

"Probably," Billy agreed. "I hope you will agree to take this case. You know as well as I do that you could always send Dudley down some dead end trail way off in the sticks where he would be out of your hair."

"I guess I could do that," Longarm admitted.

"Of course you could. And, if you could capture or kill the murderers, you'd be a hero."

"That kind of thing doesn't matter to me."

"What *does* matter to you besides women and whiskey?"

Longarm smiled wryly. "Just bringing outlaws and killers to justice. Doing a job well that few men could do. Being out on my own without anyone looking over my shoulder and telling me how to do things. I need to work for myself and being on assignment comes close to meeting that need."

Billy nodded with understanding. "I can remember what it was like. Some of the best times—but also the worst—were when I wore a badge and was on assignment. There's a freedom out there that I've lost in this office."

"So take a demotion!"

Billy smiled a little sadly. "You know I'd never do that because of my family. I've traded my freedom for something even more precious."

"There's nothing more precious to a man than his freedom," Longarm said. "But you do have a wonderful family and I understand."

"See you tomorrow mid-afternoon," Billy told him as he lit his corncob pipe. "Until then, stay sober and stay out of trouble."

"You know that I will."

"Still dating that tall blonde named Honey?"

"Yep."

"I thought you told me you were going to part company because she was pushing you so hard to get married."

Longarm shrugged. "She's backed off that a bit. And besides, she's too lovable to easily forget."

"Best looking woman in Denver," Billy said a little wistfully, then caught himself and quickly added, "except for my wife."

"Oh sure." Longarm chuckled and shut the door as he headed down the hallway.

"Hey, Custis!"

Longarm turned to see Mack hurrying to catch up with him. The man was slovenly and slow witted. Longarm had no use for Mack but at least the deputy marshal was honest and hardworking.

"Custis, I heard that you have something important to do in Reno."

"Maybe."

"And I also heard that you might need a partner."

8

"Could be."

"If so, I'd like to volunteer. I like Nevada. And we would make a hell of a team. So what's the deal?"

"Beats me," Longarm told the man. "All I know is that people are being murdered out there."

"Then let's put a damn quick stop to that!" Mack shouted. "We'll shoot first and ask questions later. We'll put the fear of the gawd and the law in their murderin' hearts, by jingo!"

"Sorry," Longarm said, wanting to get away from the man. "But I've been asked to pair up with some fella from Boston."

"Boston!" Mack shouted. "Holy cow! Now why would they do a thing like that to you?"

"I haven't a clue."

"Maybe I'll go have a powwow with Billy and see if I can pound some good sense into him. You need a partner like me. A fella that has been tested tried and true."

"You're absolutely right," Longarm said, feeling a tinge of meanness. "Why don't you go in and have a word with Mr. Vail."

"By gawd, I'll do it right now! I'll give him the facts. Show him the light of truth."

As he headed on down the hall and out of the Federal District Building on Denver's busy Colfax Avenue, it was all that Longarm could do not to burst out laughing. Deputy Marshal Mack Wilson would drive poor Billy half crazy before he was finally sent packing. And maybe, given what Longarm was being asked to do, that was only fair.

In the meantime, he had twenty-four hours of freedom and he was thinking that he might just drop in and spring Honey from her job at the Lone Pine Café. That shouldn't be too difficult seeing as how she was the owner and was always looking for an excuse to turn things over to her employees and enjoy a little fun and romance.

Billy thinks she's the best looking woman in Denver. Hmmm. I expect that is true and I'm the only one that gets to see what all of her looks like!

And so, without conscious thought, Longarm began to walk faster with the prospect of good loving filling his mind.

Chapter 2

When Longarm walked into the Lone Pine Café, Honey was sitting on a stool engaged in animated conversation with a customer. The guy she was talking to was trying to keep his eyes off her chest but wasn't having much luck.

"Hey, Honey!" Longarm called from the doorway. "Guess what?"

She gave him her usual radiant smile. Honey was a tall Scandinavian type with golden hair and perfect teeth. She was strong and had a wonderful disposition. Honey loved to make love and was kind, giving and . . . boring. She was, in fact, so boring that any serious or prolonged conversation was impossible. But so what? When a woman like Honey loved a man, who needed to talk.

"Hi, Custis!" she said, forgetting her customer and coming over to give him a powerful hug and a kiss that made his heart beat fast and his pants fill out in the most embarrassing place. "What are you doing out free and running around at this time of the day?"

"I got the afternoon off."

She beamed. "You do?"

"Yes. And I was hoping you could tie that apron on

one of your people and then we'd go do something fun." He winked. "Whatever feels right."

Honey giggled and hugged him again, this time so hard that Longarm felt his ribs crunch. "That sounds like fun to me."

"Thought it might."

Honey dashed back into her kitchen and Longarm heard her giving instructions on how to close up for the evening.

"Lucky stiff," the envious customer complained. "Some fellas get all the breaks."

"Sorry to have interrupted your ogling," Longarm told him. "But you can always go over to the red-light district and see what you were hungering for in the flesh."

"Yeah, I know. But sometimes it is more fun to imagine. Know what I mean, Marshal?"

"No."

The customer sighed. "If I was six-foot-four like you and still handsome instead of ugly as a barnyard mutt, I'd make a play for Honey."

"You could try," Longarm told him. "But then I'd have to have words with you and, if necessary, pound some sense and good manners into that thick head."

"I guess you would at that," the man whose name Longarm had forgotten said. "Anyway, I'm engaged to be married."

"Then you shouldn't be having thoughts of Honey."

"Have to be brainless not to."

"I suppose."

"Since you are engaged to be married, perhaps you shouldn't come around here anymore."

"That's good advice. But my fiancée is skinny as the handle of a broom and kinda ugly."

"Well, at least you won't ever have to be jealous."

"I don't guess I will," he conceded. Draining his coffee, the customer laid a dime on the counter and headed for the door muttering, "Lucky stiff."

"Stiff *and* lucky," Longarm corrected, causing the man to laugh out loud.

"Let's go," Honey said, slipping her arm around Longarm's waist. "It's a fine day out and I'd sure enjoy a stroll along the river."

"Later we might just find time to do that," he told her. "But first, I sort of had other ideas."

Honey looked up at his handsome, grinning face and laughed. "Sometimes, Custis, I think you do have a one-track mind."

"I'm sure you're right," he told her as they headed for Honey's house only two blocks away.

Longarm wasn't a man to waste time with the preliminaries. Besides, Honey wasn't a woman who need much warming up in preparation to make passionate love. So they both headed straight for her bedroom and tore off their clothes.

"Oh my," he said, eyes filled with admiration, "you are built to make love."

She giggled. "Maybe also to make babies. You'd make a wonderful father, Custis."

"No, I wouldn't."

"I disagree." Honey came over and snuggled up against Longarm, causing his member to rise and throb with anticipation. She took it in her hand and then knelt and took it in her mouth.

"Oh," Longarm sighed, lacing his fingers into her hair and pulling her face close. "You *are* good!"

Honey's tongue laved his swollen member and her lips teased his desire until Longarm was trembling. "It's time," he whispered.

Honey stood and went over to the bed. "How would you like me?"

"I'll take you from behind," he said, his voice hoarse with desire.

13

"I like it that way, too." Honey climbed onto the bed staying on her hands and knees. She looked back as Longarm pushed himself up tight against her bottom. "Come on, big boy. I'm hot and ready."

Longarm reached around her belly and his finger found her bud of passion. She was wet and he caressed the center of her desire until she was squirming and bumping hard against him.

"Don't make me wait any longer," she pleaded and moaned. "Put it in *now* before I go crazy!"

Longarm was only too happy to oblige and began to push his huge rod slowly into her body, one tantalizing inch at a time. Her bottom began to quiver and she bucked trying to engulf him quickly, but Longarm made her wait a few moments before he filled her eager womanhood.

"Take me like a stallion does a mare in heat," she breathed. "Hard and fast."

"Whatever you want," he said. "We can do it slow later."

Longarm took her hips in his big hands and began to slam them back and forth, each time impaling Honey harder and deeper. His hips moved forward as hers moved back and, when they met, both of them gasped with pleasure. Then, without explanation, he slowed and began to grind in circles against her firm buttocks.

Honey threw her head back and groaned. "You're driving me mad!"

"All right," he panted as his rod began to piston in and out of her honey pot. "Like this better?"

"Oh, do I!" she cried, dropping her head down and watching his great member slide in and out of her wetness.

When Longarm heard her familiar squeals and felt her start bucking again, he knew that Honey was ready to reach the height of her passion. Gripping her even more

14

firmly, his lips drew back from his teeth and his eyelids shuttered.

"Yes!" she cried, pounding the mattress with a clenched fist and then tossing her head back and howling with pleasure.

Longarm knew the moment was at hand. He clenched his teeth and began pumping like a wild horse until he shouted and filled her with his hot, spurting seed.

They lay wet and satisfied on the bed that night after another long session of lovemaking. "So how long will you be gone this time?" she asked.

"I have no idea."

"I wish you didn't have to take the greenhorn kid, but I suppose some help is better than *no* help."

He stared up at the ceiling. "I'm afraid that is not true. In a crisis, if I have to worry about an amateur, then I won't be able to focus all my attention on what needs to be done."

"Then why don't you just lose the Boston boy when you reach Nevada?"

"I've thought of that," Longarm admitted. "But then I'd be in even hotter water with the director. And besides, this kid would probably telegraph the office. No, the best thing for me to do is to put him someplace where he thinks he is going to be doing some good . . . but where he's simply out of harm's way."

Honey snuggled closer. Her hands moved up and down her body and she shivered, remembering how he'd taken her again and again that afternoon and how they would probably make love at least a couple of more times before they said their farewells. And when Longarm returned, what a passionate time they would have again! Honey hated to see him go . . . but it did bring out the animal in them both.

"Let's sleep for a while," Longarm said with a yawn.

"Okay, but . . . if I get hungry for you—"

"Then wake me and we'll see what I have left down there to give," he told her with a laugh.

"What you have to give is a whole lot of man," Honey replied, closing her eyes and falling asleep almost at the same time.

They both slept until morning, then made love before getting up and strolling down to her café for a hearty breakfast. As they entered her café, Honey caught her reflection in the window and whispered, "My cheeks are really rosy and my lips are swollen."

"No one will notice."

"Yes, they will." Honey giggled. "And I'll bet they can guess why we are both walking a little bowlegged this morning."

"Shhh!" he said, trying not to smile.

When the breakfast was over and they had enjoyed all the coffee they could stand, Honey said, "Why don't we go for a walk before we say our good-byes."

"That sounds good," Longarm agreed.

"Let's go walking along Cherry Creek."

"Whatever you like."

Cherry Creek was only a block away and they had often strolled along its tree-covered paths, sometimes walking up to where it joined the South Platte River. Honey loved water and Longarm supposed it had something to do with her nationality. She was Danish and the Danes were a seafaring people . . . so she said.

As they strolled along together, Honey's arm resting lightly on his arm, Longarm thought about how much he was dreading his upcoming assignment. That bothered him because he was usually excited about going to faraway places and taking on the most difficult cases. And this case certainly did sound challenging. Random murders were always the most difficult to solve. In all of his years of working as a United States Deputy Marshal,

Longarm had only come across two cases where killings were random without seemingly any rhyme or reason.

A man who loved killing for the pure joy of the killing itself was a savage and heartless creature that needed to either be imprisoned at once, or else killed.

"Custis?"

"Yes."

"You sure are the quiet one. What are you thinking about?"

He didn't want her to know his real concern so he said, "I was thinking about our making love last night. It sure was good."

She beamed. "It was better than good. But I have to ask you a question."

"Sure."

"If you . . . impregnated me . . . would you marry me and be the father of our child?"

The question startled Longarm so badly that he pulled up short. Gulping, he looked down at the beautiful woman and asked, "You aren't pregnant, are you?"

"No."

He expelled a sigh of relief. "Thank heavens!"

"But I would like to know if you would marry me or not."

"Can't we talk about something else? This is such a fine day and—"

"Custis, this is important to me. I mean . . . I know that you don't want to be tied down. I accept that fact. In fact, I even admire your independence. But if we created a child . . . well, I'd want him to have his own father and I believe you would be a good one."

"Honey, I—"

"Don't make this complicated," she said, her eyes very serious as she looked up into his face. "A simple yes—or no—will do. I want you to be very honest."

"I never gave the matter any thought."

17

"You should. It happens all the time. Why, don't you remember how that girl I hired a couple of months ago got pregnant out of wedlock? She was a real sweet girl and the cad that she was dating dropped her like a hot potato the moment that he found out she was carrying his child. I think that was terrible."

"I do, too. I remember Maggie very well. What became of her?"

"She went to Chicago to stay with her parents. They were going to be very upset but she knew they'd forgive her. I took Maggie to the train. She was crying and feeling so bad. But I told her everything would work out fine and I gave her a hundred dollars. I told her to have the child and then decide whether she wanted to keep the baby or give it up for adoption. Maggie said she'd come back to Denver because she didn't like living back East."

"You were very generous," Longarm said, meaning it. "And I suppose she was not the first unmarried girl you've had get in a family way."

"No, it wasn't. And I'm not that different from poor Maggie when it comes to getting pregnant. So I need to know if you would marry me and be our child's father."

"I would," he said.

Honey threw her arms around his neck. "I just knew you wouldn't abandon me!"

"No," he said, "but I'm not sure that I would quit my job and stay at home. You see, I get kind of restless after a few weeks here. And the thought of being office-bound makes me almost queasy in the stomach."

"There are plenty of outdoor jobs you could find. Maybe you could even get on with the local marshal's office."

"Maybe," he said, "but I'd still be stuck in Denver all the time."

Honey's smile faded. "You're telling me that you will always be a rolling stone that gathers no moss."

18

"That's about the size of it," he admitted. "At least until I get gray hair and arthritis."

"That means you wouldn't be much of a husband or a father."

"I'm afraid that I would not."

Honey's eyes filled with tears. "Well," she said, "in that case, I'm afraid I have a confession."

"I'm listening."

"You've heard of Bill Lamont, haven't you?"

"Sure. He's a rich fella that owns lots of businesses in town."

"That's right. He wants to buy my property and put up a hotel."

"Really?"

"Yes. He's offered me quite a lot of money."

"Maybe you should accept the offer and buy a lot somewhere else in town," Longarm told her. "Your customers would follow you anyplace."

"I know that. Bill has been coming around for weeks trying to get me to sell. But I refused over and over. That only made him more persistent. And finally . . . well . . . he had other matters in mind."

Longarm leaned forward. "What 'other matters'?"

"He says he fell in love with me and wants me to be his wife."

"No!"

Her blue eyes widened. "Do you find that so difficult to believe?"

"Why of course not! You're beautiful, generous, kind and loving. But he's a really rich guy and probably says that to all the attractive women, hoping to get them into bed. It's a line as old as the hills."

Honey reached into her pocket. "I was afraid that you'd say something like that," she said quietly. "Would you marry me today?"

"What!"

"Never mind," she said, bringing a small jewelry box out of her pocket and then opening it to reveal a huge diamond ring. "Bill gave me this as an engagement ring. I've never worn it, hoping that if I gave you an ultimatum, you'd ask me to be your wife."

"Honey, don't—" Longarm swallowed hard. "You've really thrown me off center."

"I know and I'm sorry, but I had to find out."

"What?"

"If it was just . . . well, making love that brought you back to me."

"Of course not!"

"Yes it is," she said, slipping on the ring with tears spilling down her cheeks. "Good-bye, darling. We've had wonderful times, but I don't want to wind up like poor Maggie."

"She was just a kid. You've got a business and a—"

Honey pressed her fingers to his lips. "Shhh. I love you, Custis. I always will love you. But I am tired of people whispering about us behind my back and making snide little remarks about how you must be having a great time screwing me half crazy."

"Well, I do and I thought you were enjoying it as much as I was."

She gave him a sad smile. "Bill Lamont is serious and he is a good man. Of course, he isn't nearly as handsome or exciting as you are, but he tells me he wants to have a lot of kids. And actually, so do I."

"So you've decided to marry the rich man."

"I did just this minute." She smoothed his face with her fingers. "I don't care about his money. I really don't care about that at all. But I'm tired of being alone most evenings and—"

"You don't have to say anything more. I understand. You can't change what you really want and neither can I."

"So this is it."

He nodded. "Send me a wedding invitation."

"No," she told him. "It would hurt too much to see you at our wedding and it wouldn't be fair to Bill. Good-bye, Custis."

"Good-bye."

She walked away quickly. Longarm heard her sob, and it was all he could do not to rush after Honey and tell her that he'd changed his mind and would marry her. But then it would be a rash decision that he would undoubtedly come to regret.

So he let her go and, deep in his heart, wished her health, happiness, and many fine, strong children.

Chapter 3

Billy Vail did a double take when he glanced up from his correspondence and saw Longarm standing just inside his doorway. "Geez, what's wrong with you?"

"What do you mean?"

"I mean that you look awful!"

Longarm glanced down at his length. "Did I forget to put on my pants or button my fly?"

"No. Your face. You look as if you've aged ten years since yesterday."

"I didn't sleep too well last night."

"Yeah, a woman built like Honey will do that to a man," Billy said, relaxing. "So you made love all night and you are dead on your feet today."

"Something like that."

"You ought to marry her."

"That's what she told me."

Billy shook his head. "And of course, you declined."

"That's right."

"You're a damned fool. Where are you going to find a woman that looks and *acts* like a love goddess?"

"I have no idea."

Billy rose from his desk and came over to stand beside

Longarm. "Something is *really* wrong. What happened? Did you wear your pecker out and it fell off?"

"Hell, no!" Longarm responded, feeling insulted. "Honey is going to marry that rich fella whose name you see in the papers all the time. His name is Bill Lamont."

"Well I'll be damned! Lucky bastard."

"Yeah," Longarm groused. "Fame, fortune, and now Honey. I'll bet he sleeps with a big smile on his face."

"If he sleeps at all once he's married to that woman." Billy returned to his desk. "You've nobody to blame but yourself, Custis. I warned you that a woman like that wouldn't settle for being your ever-faithful mistress. So was I right . . . or was I right?"

"Let's change the subject. Is Dud here yet?"

"Yeah. We had lunch and he had to go down to the accounting department and fill out some forms. I told him to come back up here and meet you as soon as he was finished with the paperwork."

"Is he as bad as we feared?"

Billy laced his hands behind his head. "Actually, I think you will be pleasantly surprised. He's a hell of a good-looking rascal and seems to be modest and willing to learn. He admits that he is pretty green but is willing to learn."

"Let's just hope he has time to learn before someone out here puts a bullet hole in his head."

"Yeah, let's," Billy agreed.

They talked awhile longer and then were interrupted by a firm knock on Billy's door. He winked at Longarm and hollered, "Come on in!"

Dudley L. Applewhite stepped into the office and Longarm had to admit that he'd sold the kid short. Dudley was almost as tall as himself, square-jawed and broad-shouldered, too. He was as clean-cut and as handsome as an actor, and when he smiled, he had the most perfect and whitest set of teeth that Longarm had ever seen.

"Deputy Marshal Long," the kid said, striding across the room with his outstretched hand, "it is a real pleasure to meet you."

That would have been a good start, except that Dudley caught his toe in the throw rug on Billy's polished floor and took a hard fall. His head bounced off the wood and, for a moment, he must have seen stars because when Longarm knelt by his side, the kid's eyes were closed and he was unconscious.

"Oh my gawd!" Billy exclaimed. "He cracked his skull! In *my* office!"

Longarm slapped Dud's pink cheeks, once on each side. Dud's eyes popped open and he struggled to rise to his feet.

"Take it easy, Dud," Longarm ordered, holding him down. "You had a bad spill there and really cracked your noggin hard. Just give yourself a moment or two and take deep breaths."

Dudley Applewhite took three deep breaths and his vision cleared. "I'm okay now. I'd like to get up, please."

Big, strong and handsome with good manners. Clumsy, though, Longarm thought, releasing the kid.

"I can't believe I did that," Dudley said, slumping into a vacant chair. He bent his head over and cradled it between his palms. "Oh, man, I sure hit hard."

"Are you seeing double?" Longarm asked hopefully, knowing that might mean a doctor would prohibit him from travel.

Dudley raised his head and stared at them. He closed one eye, then the other. "No."

"Damn," Longarm whispered under his breath.

"I'll get you a drink of water . . . or would you rather have a cup of coffee?" Billy asked, leaping toward the door.

"Water would be good."

"I'll be right back." He cast a hard glance at Longarm. "Why don't you two get acquainted?"

"Sure," Custis said in a dispirited tone of voice.

"Marshal Long, I'm sure sorry."

"About what? Catching your toe on the rug and taking that spill? Heck, everyone has done that a time or two."

"Yeah, I suppose."

"Are you *sure* you're all right?"

"I'll be just fine. I've taken a knock or two in my time. My father was a bare knuckles fighter, you know."

"Is that right?"

"Sure, and he almost won a belt. Would have, except the man he fought for the title cheated."

"How'd he do that?"

"Hit my father in the balls. He was a short guy and he had a wicked uppercut. Knew right where to explode the old family jewels."

"Tough break," Longarm replied. "Did he teach you anything about fighting?"

Dudley brightened. "As a matter of fact, he did!" The kid's chin came up and he shook his head. "I could have made the boxing team at Harvard but I wanted to get out in the West and experience life. So I got appointed a federal marshal and here I am."

"Just like that."

"Yep. And I hear that we are going to Reno to crack a murder ring."

" 'A murder ring'?"

"Sure. I read the file this morning and I've got it all figured out."

"Oh, do you now?" Longarm said, lacing his fingers behind his head and studying Dudley with sudden interest. "Exactly what have you figured out?"

"Well," Dudley said, "the crimes have all the marks of a pair of crazies. We had a couple like that in Boston, and I'd be willing to bet that these murders were committed

26

by just such a pair. They were the Hoggins brothers and you've never come across a more bloodthirsty pair."

"Really?"

"That's right," Dudley said. "The police finally apprehended them when they tried to make off with the head of their latest victim. Now I know you're going to ask me why they would put a human head in a pillowcase, but I can't answer that. They were evil and bestial, and who knows what were their bloody intentions."

Longarm nodded in agreement. "So you think that we have a pair of murdering and sadistic brothers running wild in Reno?"

"Oh," Dudley said, "they might not be brothers. But you know how birds of a feather flock together. They might just be friends but from what I've read, it's clear that robbery is not their primary motive. No sir. If that were true, they wouldn't mutilate and torture their victims before robbing them. Do you agree?"

Actually, Longarm did agree and he was wishing he'd have taken an hour yesterday to read the files before rushing off to bed Honey. No, on second thought, he'd done the right thing. "So, Dud, how do you think we're going to find and arrest these sick bastards?"

"Lucky," he corrected. "I like to be called by my nickname. Lucky."

Longarm's congeniality evaporated. "Let's get something straight, Dud. I call you Dud until you prove to me you are more help than hindrance. I didn't ask for a partner . . . even a seasoned veteran. I never work with a partner and I damn sure didn't want no greenhorn to worry about, so the sooner you understand that what I say goes . . . the better we'll get along."

Dudley sat up straighter. "Are you always such a crabby sonofabitch, or is it just something about me that is making you that way?"

The question caught Longarm completely off guard and

he burst out laughing just as Billy rushed in with a glass of water. "Did I miss a good joke?"

"No," Dudley said. "This big horse's ass just laid down the law on me and I wanted to know what his problem was. But he laughed."

Billy threw a hard glance at Longarm. "What's so funny?"

"Dud has some gumption," Longarm said. "I had him figured to burst out in tears if I challenged him and got firm but, instead, he got angry."

"I don't like to be talked to like a kid. And I don't like tõ be laughed at, either." Dudley came to his feet, hands clenched into fists. "Maybe we ought to step out in the back of this building and settle our differences."

"Sit down," Longarm ordered with a smile. "We're not going anywhere right now."

Dudley took his seat, but he glared at Longarm. "If you aren't willing for me to go along with you, then say so right now and I'll make other plans."

"That's not necessary," Billy assured the young man.

"Oh yeah? What plans?" Longarm asked with sudden interest.

"Well," Dudley replied. "There must be other cases that I could be assigned to. I was hoping to work with the best, but I didn't realize he was going to be such a shit-head."

Longarm's voice took on an edge. "Are you calling me—"

"Yeah, I am!" Dudley shouted coming out of his chair, fists knotted and jaw clenched.

Longarm stood up. Eye to eye, the kid and the veteran appraised each other with strong dislike.

"Sit down, both of you!" Billy shouted, jumping up from his desk and pushing between the two much bigger and stronger men. "Do you hear me!"

They sat.

"Are we professionals or not?" Billy ranted. "I can't believe what I'm seeing here. Custis, you're the veteran and I hold *you* responsible."

"Dud is a hothead and clumsy besides," Longarm replied, not taking his eyes off the Boston boy. "This isn't going to work out between us."

"It had better work!"

"I'm leaving for Reno in the morning," Longarm growled, coming to his feet. "I'll take the file on this case with me and read all about it on the train."

"I'm leaving for Reno on the same train," Dudley snapped. "If you won't work with me, then I'll crack the case on my own just to make you look like the fool you are."

Longarm desperately wanted to grab the kid by his fancy shirt collar, drag him outside, and beat him to a pulp, but he knew that would get him fired, so he barged out of the office and marched down the hall.

"Custis, come back here!" Billy shouted.

But Longarm paid his old friend no mind. Sure, Dudley L. Applewhite had some grit and courage, but, in his case, that would be a liability. A fool kid like that would mouth off to someone on the Comstock or in some cowboy saloon and he'd be riddled with bullets or slit open with a Bowie knife before he could react.

"I'll take no responsibility for him," Longarm hissed on his way down the hallway.

"You forgot the file!" Billy shouted. "Will you stop a minute!"

Longarm came to a halt. Billy caught up with him and jammed a manila envelope into his gut. "I can't believe you two," the marshal said, his face flushed with anger and unaccustomed exertion. "Two grown men acting like—"

"*One* grown man and one wet-behind-the-ears boy."

29

"Custis, if you value our friendship, then I expect you to take care of Dudley Applewhite."

"He's too young and inexperienced for this job and he's way too old to be nursemaided by the likes of me."

"He's got a temper, but so do you."

"He won't listen to me."

"No," Billy corrected, "he just won't allow you to call him 'Dud' or 'kid', both of which are insulting."

"Be damned if I'll call him Lucky."

"Then call him by his real name . . . Dudley."

"All right," Longarm said. "If I see him out west, that's what I'll do."

Billy grabbed Longarm by the shirtsleeves. "Listen, I really want you to help this kid."

"Why? Because he has some connections? Billy, can't you see that the best thing we could possibly do for Dudley is to send him packing? And while that might bruise some feelings it would sure be the merciful and wise thing to do. That kid won't cut the mustard out west."

"He's not afraid to try."

"Tell him to go to Harvard and learn to box like a gentleman," Longarm said tersely.

"He's going to Reno on the same train that you are," Billy replied. "And I expect you to work together to solve these murders."

"And what if I refuse?"

"Then we might both be out of a job."

Longarm swore under his breath and the thick file of telegrams and newspaper clippings crumpled in his fists. But he nodded his head. "All right, Billy. But I'll send him off someplace doing something that I think will keep him out of harm's way."

"Thank you!"

"You're welcome."

"Now come back to the office and make up."

"Not a chance." Longarm took a deep breath. "Tell him

that I'll call him Dudley and that I'll see him on the train early tomorrow morning."

"And that you've agreed to work with him."

"Yeah."

Billy heaved a deep sigh of relief. "Sometimes," he said, "I wish . . . oh, never mind."

"What?"

"I wish that I had become a mule skinner?"

"Why?"

"Because," Billy said, "I am getting to be very knowledgeable about jackasses—the two-legged kind."

Longarm had to smile at that. He clamped his hand on Billy's shoulder and squeezed it hard. "Just tell the kid that I got jilted by the most beautiful woman in Denver. Tell him that was what was really sticking in my craw."

"Sounds like an apology."

"It's not, but it's the truth," Longarm told his friend.

"Custis, it might not be too late to mend your fences with Honey."

"It is too late."

"I doubt that. Seems to me that, if she loved Mr. Lamont, she'd never have agreed to go to bed with you last night. I think you're the one that she really loves."

"Maybe, but she's as much as gave me an ultimatum. Marry her or hit the road."

"Tough choice all right. It's one that I had to face when I was about your age. I chose to marry my wife and I've never regretted that choice."

"Oh, bullshit! You're always complaining to me about being deskbound and about having to play office politics."

"True, but I am by nature a complainer. I complained just as much when I had your job."

"For a fact?"

"Yes. I like to complain."

"Well I don't," Longarm told him. "And I am not ready

31

to settle down and be a husband and a father. Did I ever tell you that you smelled like baby poop for about the first year after your kid was born?"

"Yes, you did," Billy snapped. "But I didn't care."

"I would." Longarm patted his paunchy friend on the shoulder. "Look. I'm sorry about what happened in here and you're right . . . I am the veteran and I should have handled the situation better. Tell the kid that I'll be feeling more . . . friendly, after I've had a few drinks tonight at O'Malley's Saloon."

"Don't get so drunk that—"

"I'll be at the train on time."

"I'll meet you and Dudley there with your tickets and some traveling funds. I tried to get them earlier but accounting just wasn't up to the job."

"I know." Longarm turned and started back down the hall. Mack Wilson popped out of his office, grinning. "Hey, I take it you met the dude!"

"Not now," Longarm warned.

But Mack fell in step with him. "I take it from the look on your mug that you and the Boston golden boy didn't hit it off so good, huh?"

"Go find something to do."

"You want me to ask the director if I can take your place on that train tomorrow morning? I will if you want."

"Get lost, Mack."

"I kinda liked the kid. We had a cup of coffee downstairs and he seemed all right to me. I think we could team up and do one hell of a good job in Reno."

"Do whatever you want," Longarm said, shoving the deputy aside as he exited the hallway and took the stairs two at a time.

Mack yelled. "You don't have to be such a sore head!"

Longarm didn't look back and he didn't reply. He was

going to go home and pack, then go out and have a few drinks. And if anyone gave him any more trouble this awful day . . . well, he'd take real pleasure in knocking their teeth down their damned throat.

Chapter 4

O'Malley's Saloon was one of Longarm's favorite drinking holes. The owner, Mike O'Malley, was a big Irishman, who, when he was a little in his cups, could put the world's finest baritones to shame. Mike had a little leprechaun of a piano player named Clancy and the two of them would sing and play music so sweet and sad that it would make most of the patrons weep.

"Hey, Custis!" Mike shouted, beckoning him over to an empty table. "I haven't seen you around in the last few days."

"I've been sort of busy."

"You look like hell. Sit down and I'll buy you a pint of ale."

"I'd prefer whiskey."

"We have that, too," Mike bellowed. "Whiskey over here for the marshal! Bring a bottle of our best."

"Thanks, Mike."

"Say nothing of it. How come you look so sad?"

Longarm slumped down in a chair. "Honey is going to marry Bill Lamont."

"Ah," Mike said with a grimace. "That's terrible news! He ought to be hanged for stealing your best girl!"

"He didn't exactly 'steal' her away from me. Honey gave me the choice and I told her to marry the man."

Mike's lantern jaw sagged. "What!"

"She wants to have a home life . . . a family. She wants to have a bunch of kids."

Mike threw up his big hands. "Well, so what? I've got seven kids and plan to father seven more!"

"Fine for you, maybe, but that's not for me."

Mike leaned forward with a conspiratorial grin. "Don't you see, Marshal. Lots of kids means lots of humping. And with a woman like Honey . . . well, what could be finer?"

"I'm just not ready to settle down. Honey wants me to quit my job and work in town."

"And would that be so awful? Why, you could even work nights for me as a bouncer and enforcer." Mike rubbed his ruined knuckles. "I'm getting a little old for that game, but you have a lot of good years left."

"No, thanks. I like what I do right now."

"Could there be no compromise?"

"I'm afraid not. Lamont bought Honey a diamond engagement ring. I swear it must have cost him a thousand dollars. Damn diamond was the size of a robin's egg."

"Hmmm," Mike mused aloud. "Well, I know a place where you can buy a fake diamond that size for about twenty dollars. The girl would never know the difference."

"I think she might."

"I doubt it," Mike said. "And anyway, once you were hitched—"

"It's over," Longarm told him as the bartender placed a shot glass full of whiskey in front of him.

"Bring over the bottle," Mike told his bartender. "Poor Custis here lost his lady love to the likes of Bill Lamont."

The bartender, another Irishman, shook his head in commiseration. "That's a damn dirty shame! Rich men

36

always get the best-looking women. He's probably lying just to get the poor girl into his bed. He'll use her awhile and then tire of that game and move on to another poor girl with stars in her eyes and tits to make a milk cow envious."

"He's right," Mike agreed. "Mr. Lamont often comes here for a few libations and some good Irish company. He's part Irish and not all that bad of a fellow."

"He tips real well," the bartender added. "Always seems in a good mood and I've seen him bring in some real beauties . . . though none so fair as your Honey."

"She not my Honey anymore," Longarm said tightly.

"Well, you know what I meant. And if Mr. Lamont drops Honey you could step back in and—"

"Let's change the subject," Longarm said louder than intended. "I'm heading for Reno tomorrow morning, but tonight I'd just like to have a few drinks and listen to you and Clancy sing some happy Irish songs."

"There are none."

"Then sing the sad ones, if you must," Longarm said, tossing down his whiskey. "But I don't want to hear Honey's name mentioned again this evening. Is that understood?"

"Yes, sir!" Michael said, motioning for his bartender to hurry off and return with a bottle.

"Get good and drunk," the Irish saloon owner said in his kindest, most understanding voice. "It will take your mind off your misery. Tonight, you drink for free."

"You're a good friend."

"Aye, that I am. But I well remember having a woman once who looked like Honey. She jilted me." He clamped his hand to his broad chest and looked up at his water-stained ceiling. "Broke my heart just as surely as if it were a mug of ale. It took me nearly a month to get over that lassie."

"But you did."

"Oh, sure! You know, it's true when they say there are always plenty more fish in the sea and women to be bedded."

"No, thanks. I've got to get up early and catch the train."

"Ah, you can sleep on the damned train. Let me tell you something. The girl I have in mind is pretty and she really knows how to scorch the bedsheets."

"I'm just not in the mood."

"Then you must be heartbroken. Drink up and pretty soon I'll sing some songs."

"Thanks."

"Think nothing of it. The Irish are romantics. We love nothing better than to commiserate with someone whose heart is bleeding."

"My heart isn't bleeding."

"Oh, sure it is!"

"Go away," Longarm told the man with a sad smile. "I'd prefer to be left to my own company for a while."

"I understand. The lass who broke my heart the first time was named . . . Polly. Or was it Margaret? Hmmm, I kinda forget, but I do remember that I took my pistol out and cocked back the hammer, my broken heart filled with pain."

Longarm frowned. "You were actually going to shoot yourself over her?"

"Of course not! I was going to shoot *her*!"

"Oh."

"I was heartbroken, not crazy. And besides, there was another young lady that I sort of had my eye on at the time. Her name was Mary, or maybe it was Darcy. I forget. But—"

"Get out of here," Longarm repeated with half a smile.

"As you like, Marshal. As you like. But, if you need comforting words this evening, you call me as a friend and I'll listen to your sad tale of woe until the wee hours of the morning."

"Thanks, Mike."

The Irishman got up and walked away shouting, "Honey just broke the marshal's poor heart by agreeing to marry Mr. Lamont. So leave the man alone to his whiskey and his misery!"

Heads nodded. Glasses and bottles were raised in a silent toast by men convinced they knew how bad Longarm felt. But he didn't see them because his eyes were fixed on his glass and the mysteries he could read in the swirling liquid amber of Michael O'Malley's best brand of whiskey.

It was about eleven o'clock in the evening and the saloon was filled with customers. Longarm had remained at the same table all through the evening. At least a dozen of the regulars had come over to extend their condolences about losing Honey to the rich and powerful Mr. Bill Lamont. Longarm had quickly run them off, preferring to wallow in his own misery.

"Marshal," the big Irishman said, dragging along a pretty red-haired girl in her twenties, "this here is Miss Della Riley. Della, the marshal is feeling kind of down in the dumps and I thought you two ought to get acquainted."

Longarm forced a smile. He appreciated O'Malley's concern and the girl was attractive, but tonight he was mourning the loss of Honey and he wasn't interested.

"Pleased to meet ya, Marshal."

"Same here."

"Well, ask the girl to sit down and have a drink with you," O'Malley said. "You and Miss Riley have something in common."

"Oh yeah?" Longarm asked. "And what would that be?"

"I was Bill's girlfriend. He promised to marry me but the rat never did."

Longarm shook his head. Della was attractive, but she was nothing near as nice as Honey. "You were engaged to Bill Lamont?" he asked.

"Well, not exactly engaged. I mean, he never gave me no diamond or nothing, but every time we did it I made him promise to marry me. The dirty rat."

"I'm about to leave but I'd like to offer you a drink before I do."

"Much obliged, Marshal."

Della looked up at O'Malley. "You can go now. I'll be fine with the marshal."

"Is Lance still after you?" the saloon owner asked.

"Yeah, but he don't worry me."

"Who is Lance?" Longarm asked, looking first at the girl and then at the big Irishman.

"Don't worry about him," Della said. "Lance was my latest boyfriend. We broke up last a few nights ago and he swore he'd kill me if I so much as looked at another man. He's real jealous. I couldn't stand it any longer, so that's why we broke up."

"Oh," Longarm said, refilling his glass and pushing it across the table toward Della.

Longarm lit a cheroot and studied the men at the bar. He was having a little difficulty focusing.

"You're a real handsome feller," Della said, sliding his empty glass back across the table. "Too bad about Honey."

"Yeah."

"I guess we both have lost out to the high and mighty Bill Lamont. But you know what?"

"What?"

Della laid her arm on his thigh and gave him a squeeze under the table. "I say good riddance to the both of them."

"That's the attitude, all right."

"You wanna go find a room?"

"Maybe next time."

"I might have another boyfriend the next time we meet."

Longarm was just about to say that he didn't much care when he heard a man clear his throat loudly. "Marshal Long. Could I have a word with you?"

He twisted around and saw Dudley Applewhite. "Sure. Sit down. Dudley, this is Della. Della, Dudley."

"Pleased to make your acquaintance," she said, smiling sweetly. "Are you a marshal too?"

"Deputy Marshal."

"Geez, all you marshals are long, tall, and handsome fellas. Have a drink on poor old Marshal Long and me."

"Don't mind if I do," Dudley said, easing into a chair next to the young woman.

"You got a friend, Dudley?" she asked.

"Nope."

"That's *real* good 'cause I'm lookin' for a boyfriend."

Dudley gulped. "Marshal, could we step outside and have a word together in private?"

"I don't think so," Longarm replied. "I told Billy to tell you that we'd work things out, but I'd as soon start tomorrow as tonight."

"I understand. He told me about you being jilted by Honey."

Longarm ground his teeth. "Hasn't anybody in this town got any damn thing to talk about except who jilted who!"

"Well, you don't have to yell at me," Dudley said. "I came here to say I was sorry about our bad start and to say I don't hold it against you."

Della slipped her hand off Longarm's thigh and onto Dudley's thigh. "You're a very nice young man."

She started to say something else, but then her jaw

dropped and her eyes bugged. Longarm wasn't watching her but Dudley twisted around in his chair just in time to see a large, unshaven man come barging through the front door.

"Della, gawdammit, I told you—"

"Lance!"

Before anyone could react, Lance charged across the floor and would have bashed Della in the head with his fist if Dudley hadn't jumped up and stood in his path.

"Mister, you better go back where you came from," he warned, raising his fists.

Longarm leaned back in his chair, suddenly interested in his surroundings. He watched Lance turn his eyes down to see Della's hand resting on Dudley's thigh. Then with a roar, he swung at Dudley with a roundhouse right that would have knocked over a draft horse.

Dudley ducked the punch and delivered a wicked uppercut to the man's stomach. Lance's mouth flew open and he backpedaled.

"Just leave us be, mister!" the young man from Boston shouted. "We are both United States Marshals and we won't tolerate that kind of behavior!"

"That's telling him," Longarm said, nodding his head with approval.

But Lance must have hated marshals because he drew his gun and pointed it at Dudley. The crowd hit the floor and Longarm's smile melted.

"Now . . . now you don't want to use that gun," Dudley warned. "Put it back in your holster."

But Lance laughed. "You been screwin' Della, have you?"

"No, I just met her. I—"

"You're a gawdamned liar!"

Longarm eased his gun out of his holster. The table blocked it from view and he cocked the weapon, hoping he was still sober enough to shoot straight. The distance was less than twenty feet so he figured he could do the job.

"Don't shoot him, Lance! He's tellin' the truth."

"Oh, yeah!" Lance turned his gun on Della. "Then maybe you're the whore who deserves to die!"

"Marshal," Dudley hissed. "Do something!"

Longarm took a deep breath. He was seeing things in double vision so he closed one eye and shouted, "Mister, drop your gun!"

Lance swung his aim at Longarm. "You must either be dead drunk or real stupid! I'm the one holding the gun and you're doing nothin' but flappin' your gums. I hate marshals and I have just decided to kill all three of you!"

"Lance, please don't do this!"

He turned his gun back to her. "I think I'll start with *you*, Della!"

Longarm knew that the man was serious and so he yanked up his gun and fired. His first slug missed Lance and drilled a picture of a naked lady hanging on the wall. Drilled her right between the eyes. But his second shot was on target and it caught Lance about two inches below his throat, then knocked him back out the door into the street.

Della let out a cry and fainted.

Longarm reholstered his gun as every man in the crowded saloon seemed to unthaw.

"Holy mother of gawd!" O'Malley shouted. "Marshal, I thought all three of you were goners!"

Dudley's hand was shaking as he reached for the bottle of whiskey on Longarm's table. There wasn't a whole lot remaining but what there was of it, the kid poured down his throat in a series of long, shuddering swallows.

He wiped tears from his eyes, cleared his throat and said, "Marshal, you sure did kill that man."

"Well," Longarm said, "he sure did need killing."

Dudley looked down at Della. "What should we do with her?"

"Nothing. She'll be fine. I'm ready to leave. Maybe we can find a café still open and get something to eat along with some coffee."

"Are you drunk?"

Longarm stood up, swayed, and had to grab the arms of his chair to keep from falling. "I guess I about am, Dud."

"You saved my life so you can call me any damn thing you like."

"That's good," Longarm told his young companion. "Sorry I missed the first shot. That was pretty bad, given the distance."

"Maybe, but you drilled him dead center with the second shot."

"And you busted him a good one in the belly," Longarm said, throwing his arm across Dud's shoulder. "I think I saw that fella's boots come clear off the floor when you connected. I guess you weren't lying when you said you learned something about fighting from your pa."

"Maybe you can teach me how to handle a gun like you do."

"Maybe," Longarm agreed.

"Marshal!" O'Malley cried, rushing back in from the street. "That fella was a bad one and I'd like to propose a toast to you and offer drinks on the house!"

A cheer arose from the throat of every man in the saloon. But Longarm and Dudley Applewhite were already staggering out the door. They paused for a few moments to study Lance and the crowd that had gathered around his body.

"Better pass the hat," Longarm said, fumbling into his pockets and finding two silver dollars, which he threw down between the dead man's feet. "Even a jealous fool deserves a decent burial."

44

Men laughed nervously and the hat began to go around the circle. Longarm raised his hand and pointed down the street. "We can find something to eat and some coffee that'a way, partner."

"Good enough, sir!"

"Don't call me no 'sir,' " Longarm warned. "Makes me feel old and more important that I am."

"All right, Custis." They began walking. "Have you looked at the Nevada file of murders yet?"

"Nope."

"Well, I have some new ideas I've been working on."

"Let's hear them on the train," Longarm said. "I am sick and tired of talking about women, killing, and Bill Lamont."

"Who is he?"

"He's the man that my woman is going to marry."

"Oh. I'm sorry."

"Don't matter anymore," Longarm told his young friend. "Women come and women go."

"Were you taking a liking to Della?"

Longarm chuckled. "Not quite, but I might have on some other night."

"She was pretty but kind of dumb, I think."

In response, Longarm began to laugh out loud.

Chapter 5

Longarm had slept for two days after boarding the Denver Pacific up to Cheyenne and then the Union Pacific across Wyoming. They'd seen the distant Great Salt Lake and then the harsh and nearly waterless deserts of northern Nevada.

"I never imagined this country could be so big and so empty," Dudley commented for maybe the hundredth time. "Back east where I come from there are trees most everywhere. You don't get these kinds of vistas. I feel almost . . . exposed out here."

Longarm frowned and looked up at the young man sitting across from him. " 'Exposed'?"

"Yeah, you know. Kinda like a bug all alone on a tabletop. I keep looking up and wondering if something is going to come diving out of the sky to pluck me up in its talons."

"That's kinda strange, Dud."

The Sierra Nevada Mountains could now be seen, hazy and blue in the distance. Longarm stretched and said, "We should be in Reno within two hours."

"Good! So how are we going to handle this case?"

Longarm's brow furrowed and he stared at the window

as if giving the matter some deep and serious thought. Finally, he said, "I think the best way to solve this murder case is to work independently and undercover."

"Huh?"

"Look," Longarm explained as if it were elemental. "If we hide our badges and assume false identities, then we can cover a lot more ground by operating apart."

"But—"

"Now hear me out," Longarm said, raising his index finger. "I do think it's important that we keep in touch."

"Well, of course we should!"

"But we also need to act like strangers."

Longarm could see that Dudley was having a tough time with this line of thinking, but he wanted to make sure that Dudley stayed out of harm's way.

"Well, what the deuce am I supposed to be or do?" the Boston kid asked, looking confused.

"That's an excellent question." Longarm thumbed the brim of his hat back a notch. "I was thinking you ought to pose as a traveling salesman."

Dudley's expression became stricken. "I can't do that!"

"Why not?"

"I . . . don't *want* to be a traveling salesman."

"Well, you need to be something that travels," Longarm insisted. "And so do I. We have to have a legitimate reason to be poking around the countryside, don't we?"

"I guess so."

"Dud, do you know anything about blacksmithing?"

"Of course not. But I do know quite a bit about horses. I had an uncle who was a horse trader. I spent summers with him and we traveled—"

"That's perfect!" Longarm exclaimed. "You can be a Nevada horse trader."

"But I don't have any money or horses!"

"Wire your family in Boston and ask for some funds," Longarm told him. "Why, if you really know horses you

48

might even make a profit while we solve this case."

"What the hell are you going to be?"

"I might be a snake oil peddler. I've always sort of admired the way they travel around in a wagon selling hope and whiskey thinly masqueraded as healing elixir."

Dudley snorted with derision. "That sounds as if it ought to be illegal."

"Maybe, but I've seen people buy that stuff and they usually feel a whole lot better."

"That's because they get drunk on the medicine."

"So what if it works and they're happy?" Longarm shrugged. "It's not like they are being taken for a lot of money. I wouldn't charge much more than the medicine costs to make. And that would give me the excuse I need to travel about anywhere I need to go."

"In an old medicine wagon?"

"Sure. I'd only need one horse and I'd keep a saddle and bridle in the wagon so I could race off if needed in a hurry. The only problem I'm going to have is finding and buying a medicine wagon."

"That might prove difficult all right."

"And it might be easy," Longarm replied. "Anyway, it sounds like we've worked this thing out pretty good."

"I'm not too sure about that." Dudley looked dejected. "I was hoping we could work closely together until we solve this case. Now, you're saying that isn't going to be possible."

"You have to make sacrifices sometimes," Longarm said, voice softening. "And we can meet once a week or—"

" 'Once a week!' "

"All right, every few days if we are in the same area. The thing of it is, we have to be convincing." Longarm slapped Dudley on the shoulder. "Cheer up! Every horse trader I ever knew had a great time. You'll meet some lonely and love-starved women."

"You mean—"

Longarm winked. "All sorts of good things can happen. Why, we'll be covering the famous Comstock Lode as well as the farms and ranches around Reno and Carson City. It will be an experience of a lifetime."

"I just hope no one catches on to our trick and the experience doesn't turn into the *end* of a lifetime."

"It won't," Longarm promised. "We just have to keep our noses and ears to the ground. Sooner or later, we'll get a lead and then we'll close in on the killer."

"Yeah," Dudley said, brightening a bit. "And won't that be something."

"Yes it will," Longarm agreed as he turned toward the window feeling like a scoundrel for being so deceitful to this honest, decent young man. But what he was doing was for Dudley's benefit . . . as well as his own.

Longarm had been to Reno a number of times and had always enjoyed his stay there. He liked the way the eastern slope of the mighty Sierras seemed to lean over the town and how the clear and swift Truckee River flowed right through the center of the city. Reno had more than its share of nightlife, although it had been eclipsed by the fabulously rich Comstock Lode just a few miles to the southwest.

"Marshal Long!"

Custis had been about to jump down from the train but Dudley's voice brought him up short. "Yeah?"

"Are we splitting up already?"

"Well, we can't be seen together. Someone might make the connection."

"But I don't even know where to stay tonight! Or who to talk to or how to go about acting like a horse trader."

Longarm could see the kid's point and realized that he'd have to oversee Dudley for a day or two until he gained a bit of confidence. "All right, then. We'll pretend to bump into each other at the Washoe Hotel on Virginia Street."

"The Washoe Hotel?"

"That's right. You can't miss it. It's a big two-story brick hotel right near the bridge that crosses over the river. I'll meet you there this evening and then we can pretend to meet and have dinner together in a fine little restaurant just a block south."

"Good! Shall I try and buy a horse or two?"

Longarm frowned. "Why don't you let that wait for a few days until you've sort of sized things up and put your ear to the air, so to speak."

"You mean see if I can learn about the murders."

"Exactly. The best place to do that is in the saloons, of course. You just buy a few beers for yourself and listen. Now and then, you casually ask or make a comment about the previous murders and see if that arouses interest. If it does, then you pretend to be interested, but not too interested. Got it?"

"I guess."

Longarm gave the kid a smile. "You'll catch on quick enough. You'll make a few acquaintances and then you're on your way."

"You make it sound pretty easy."

"It's not, but since most people like to talk more than listen, it's not too hard to pick up information. It also helps if you can buy a few beers for the boys."

"I see. And what are you going to do?"

"I might go up to the Comstock Lode and start poking around to see what I can discover. And buying a few beers for anyone who sounds like they know something about the murders."

"Have you even read the file yet?" Dudley asked, sounding exasperated.

"No, but I'm about to."

"You sure are taking your time."

51

"Well," Longarm replied a bit peevishly, "what good would reading it on the train have accomplished?"

"Nothing, I guess. Good luck to you, Marshal."

"Same to you," Longarm said, jumping down to the depot landing with his baggage.

He didn't look back at Dudley Applewhite because he knew the greenhorn would be standing at the train station looking lost and forlorn. But tonight, they'd pretend to meet and then Longarm would give him some more encouragement before cutting him loose. Then, it was all up to the kid. If he was resourceful and willing, Dudley might even be able to come up with some valuable information. If not, he might become discouraged and simply board the train and head back to Boston or Denver. Either way, he'd be safe and Longarm would have no reason to feel guilty.

He should have gone to college anyway, Longarm thought as he headed for the Washoe Hotel.

Longarm checked into an upstairs room and quickly thumbed through the file of unsolved murders. There really wasn't much to learn from the information he'd been given, but he counted and the death toll was at eleven. In each case, the details were sparse, but there was enough information to show that whoever was committing the murders and thefts was not only clever, but also savage and sadistic. The bodies of the victims had all been either mutilated or shot full of bullet holes. There were no witnesses and no evidence. And in most cases, it was unclear how much, if any money had been taken.

All I've got there is an obituary column, Longarm thought. This isn't much good at all.

Much of the file had been constructed by the local marshal, a man named Ralph Benson. Longarm had visited the marshal's office each time he'd come to Reno as a professional courtesy and, on every occasion, the faces had changed. He'd learned that the rich Comstock mines hired away the local lawmen paying them superior wages for taking charge of their bullion, huge payrolls, and mine security. If Marshal Benson was anything like his predecessors, the man would be young and quite inexperienced.

I just hope he is cooperative, Longarm thought as he entered the familiar marshal's office.

A man who appeared to be in his early thirties looked up from the newspaper he'd been reading. He was of average size, wearing a red flannel shirt, brown pants, and a shiny badge. He had sandy hair, blue eyes, and a guarded smile.

"Can I help you?"

"I guess you might," Longarm said, introducing himself as a federal officer from Denver.

"Sit down, Custis," the marshal of Reno said as he folded up his newspaper.

Longarm had always believed that you could judge a man by his home or his office. In this case, he saw that Ralph Benson was an exceptionally tidy man. His desk was orderly, all the papers stacked in neat little piles, his bookshelf was dusted, and his floor was clean swept. That suited Longarm just fine. He figured that orderly people generally had orderly minds and tried to do their best in most matters.

Benson laced his fingers together in his lap. "They telegraphed me a couple of days ago that you and another deputy marshal were on their way. Where is your companion?"

Longarm really had not intended to tell this man that he had a partner, but now there seemed to be no choice but to admit to the fact. "He's getting a hotel room at the Washoe."

"And what would his name be?"

"Dudley Applewhite."

A faint trace of a smile crossed Benson's lips. "Dudley?" he asked.

"That's right. He's pretty young and green. I didn't ask for help but I got it. You see, I prefer to work alone."

"So they saddled you with a kid that doesn't know squat, huh?"

"Yeah, that's right. I told him that we ought to assume false identities. I think Dudley is going to pose as a horse trader."

"And you?"

"As a snake oil peddler. You know anyone around here that might have an old medicine wagon for sale?"

"No, but there is a livery up the street that can probably sell you what you need. Sign painters are easy to find and you shouldn't have any problem getting the snake oil. I'll just ask you to make sure that it isn't harmful to anyone's health."

"Of course not."

"And that you don't fleece the citizens too bad."

"Any profits I make will go back into whatever local charity you wish."

"I could use a pay raise, but I guess that wouldn't qualify as a charity."

"I suppose not," Longarm replied.

"They don't pay me much. I could make twice what I'm making here up on the Comstock Lode, but my wife can't stand that higher elevation. She gets the sore throat and we worry about her catching pneumonia so I work cheap here in town."

"I see." Longarm reached for a cheroot. "Mind if I smoke?"

"Actually, I do. Kinda bothers my eyes."

Longarm replaced the cigar in his coat pocket. "I read the file on the murders and I have to tell you that I didn't learn much."

"I can understand that," Benson said. "They've been

going on for over a year. It's taken almost that long before I figured out they were all related. Of course, some of them were out of my jurisdiction, having occurred on the Comstock or down around Carson City."

"I see. No wonder you didn't see the relationship. How did you tie them together?"

"The horse that the murderer rode has corrective shoes. I'm no tracker and didn't notice that until it was pointed out to me by a blacksmith who happens to be a friend and sometimes deputy. He spotted it right away. The right front hoof of the killer's horse has a bar across its base."

"Where, exactly?"

"Right at the two ends of the horseshoe so that it kind of looks like a squashed circle. My friend says that it is fairly rare."

"I expect so," Longarm said. "That's a good clue. Anything else?"

"The killer smokes his own hand-rolled cigarettes, but then half the population does the same thing. He uses brown—not white paper—and his gun is .45 caliber."

"But no one has seen him?"

Benson steepled his fingers. He was a pleasant-looking man who reminded Longarm of a lawyer or doctor rather than a lawman. He had no scars or visible signs of combat and Longarm had the feeling Ralph Benson was not going to remain a marshal for very long.

"There have been a few dubious witnesses."

"What does that mean?"

"It means that a few people who were within eyesight of the murders reported seeing a large man on a buckskin horse leaving the scene of the crime."

"Now we're really getting somewhere."

"However," Benson said, raising his index finger, "several other questionable witnesses have reported seeing a man leaving riding a sorrel."

"Well, did you compare their stories with the odd hoof-prints?"

"I tried to but found no evidence of that bar shoe."

Longarm frowned. "Then either the killer had swapped horses or the witnesses were in error."

"That's what I figured, too."

Longarm's initial excitement was dashed. "Do you think that this man has murdered anyone in town?"

"I have no idea. You see, both up on the Comstock and down here in Reno, it is not uncommon to find someone dead in an alley, especially after a Friday or Saturday night. In most cases, these people were mugged and robbed, then killed to prevent them from identifying a witness. There is often no way for me to tell who killed them."

It sounded to Longarm as if this marshal was taking murder a bit lightly. "I know there is always a lot of murder in a boomtown, but—"

"Actually," Benson said, "I managed a mercantile before I got this job. I have very little law experience. I would have stayed in the dry goods business except that the owner sold the store out from under me. The last marshal had been shot in the belly and he died. I didn't want this job but it was the only one I was offered, so here I am."

"I see," Longarm said, sizing up the man and deciding he would not be of any help whatsoever. Benson was treading water, waiting for another job. Almost *any* job.

"I wish that I could be more helpful," the marshal said with an indifferent shrug.

"You can be," Longarm told him. "First of all, don't mention to anyone that either I or Marshal Applewhite are in town and working on this murder case. I'm sure that you can see why that is so important."

"Well, I did tell Ken."

"Who is Ken?"

"The blacksmith. And, of course, my wife and her father and a couple of friends."

"Great," Longarm said, unable to hide his displeasure. "So a lot of people know that we are in town."

"No, because I wasn't sure when you were arriving."

"Then at least keep that much a secret," Longarm said with unconcealed exasperation.

"Sure," Benson said, voice turning chilly. "And remember what I said about not fleecing the locals or making them sick."

"I won't," Longarm said, heading out the door and wondering if half of Reno already knew his and Dudley's no longer so secret game.

Chapter 6

After checking into the Washoe Hotel, Dudley sat in his room for a few minutes trying to figure out how to make the best use of the next few hours. What he felt like doing was taking a nap until suppertime but he knew that wouldn't impress Marshal Custis Long.

Not that anything he could do would impress the tall, taciturn veteran lawman. Before meeting Longarm, Dudley had learned that the man he was going to Nevada with was almost a legend. Marshal Billy Vail had explained to him that Longarm wasn't particularly pleased with having to take on a partner, especially a man as young as himself who was also an easterner.

"Being only eighteen and from Boston makes you immediately suspect in Longarm's eyes," Billy had explained. "So you're just going to have to win over his trust and respect."

"I'll sure do my best," Dudley had promised. "And I certainly appreciate you pairing me up with your best law officer."

"Custis Long is that, all right," Billy Vail had assured him. "But you need to understand that he is not an easy man to get to know. He's going to be kind of unfriendly at first, but if you sort of stay out of his way and do your best, you'll be fine."

Again, Dudley had assured the Denver marshal as well as their director that he'd keep a low profile, do as he was told, and try to be of some assistance in the Nevada murder case.

But now, sitting in the Washoe Hotel, Dudley was wondering if he'd ever win Marshal Long's approval. They'd traveled side by side for over a thousand miles on the train and the veteran had revealed little of himself, or even of how he intended to crack this case.

Maybe he hasn't any better idea of how to go about solving these murders than I do, Dudley thought. Yes! That would explain his lack of a concrete plan of action. And why he doesn't want me working by his side. I'll bet that's it exactly!

This revelation made Dudley Applewhite feel considerably better. It also gave him the impetus to climb off his bed, comb his hair, wash his face, and head on downstairs. Longarm had told him that he needed some additional funds in order to buy and sell horses. All right then, Dudley decided, I'll go to the telegraph office and wire my father for money. A thousand dollars ought to be plenty.

Dudley straightened his collar and headed downstairs, thinking that it was nice to have a plan of action. Maybe after going to the telegraph office, he'd mosey over to a livery and see if he could fool the owner into thinking that he actually was a horse trader. Hellfire, he might even see a couple of horses to buy. After all, a horse trader had to have a few animals before he started traipsing around the countryside, didn't he?

He stopped at the hotel registration desk and smiled. "Remember I told you that I was a horse trader?"

"Yes, sir," the desk clerk said.

"Well, where can I find an honest livery man? I'd like

to buy some sound animals at a fair price."

"I've heard that old Salty Bates who owns the Dollar Livery is fair. He's sharp, though, and you'll have to watch your wallet."

"Thanks for the advice. And where is the telegraph office?"

The clerk gave him directions and Dudley wasted no time in finding the place. He wrote a short telegraph to his father requesting a thousand dollars and added, I AM DOING FINE HERE IN RENO. WORKING ON AN IMPORTANT CASE. WILL KEEP IN TOUCH. LOVE TO YOU AND MOM. "LUCKY."

"Who's Lucky?" the bespectacled telegraph operator asked.

"I am."

"I thought your name was Dudley Applewhite."

"It is. Lucky is my nickname. Will you just send the telegram?"

"Three dollars is the charge. It'll go out within the hour."

Dudley paid the man an extra dollar to have the money delivered to the Washoe Hotel. "Just leave it at the desk and I'll collect it there."

"Suit yourself. But what does 'working on a case' mean?"

Dudley started to explain, then changed his mind and said, "Ah, nothing."

"I saw you and that federal marshal get off the train at about the same time. Are you a lawman?"

"Can you keep a secret?"

"Sure. Secrecy is required in this business."

"Well, then," Dudley confided, "I am a federal marshal."

"You look awful young."

"I know. I know. But maybe that will work in my favor.

I am here to help capture whoever is murdering innocent people in this area."

"You are?" The telegraph operator looked dubious. "No offense, Mr. Applewhite or Dudley or Lucky or whatever you want to be called, but you hardly look like someone the feds would send. But that other big jasper, well, I've seen him before. He's called 'Longarm,' ain't he?"

"Yes."

"I've heard that, once he's on an outlaw's back trail, the man might just as well throw up his arms and surrender."

"I suppose that is true." Dudley leaned close and whispered, "He chose me to work with him because I have my own reputation back east, you know."

"Already? At your young age?"

"Yes," Dudley said. "I was tracking down fugitives when I was sixteen years old. A bounty hunter, you know and . . . if I do say so myself, one of the best."

"For a fact!" The telegraph operator stepped back and studied the young dandy. He'd seen hundreds of men come and go and many of them were liars and braggarts, but this young fella had the size and the look of a man who spoke the truth. "Well, this here will be our little secret."

"That's what I wanted to hear."

"My lips are locked, Marshal. You couldn't pry 'em apart with a pair of hoof nippers. And good luck with the horse trading!"

Dudley straightened his coat and headed on down toward the livery. He could feel the telegraph operator watching him and knew that the older man was envious. Well, not everyone can be a famous lawman, he thought. And even if I'm not exactly famous yet . . . I soon will be when I solve this murder case either with Longarm's help . . . or without it.

The Dollar Livery was easy enough to find and Salty

Bates was a filthy old reprobate who never stopped chewing and spitting tobacco. Once, he almost spat on Dudley's shiny boots . . . would have if he hadn't jumped sideways.

"So you're a horse trader," Salty said, not bothering to hide his disbelief. "And I'm the tooth fairy."

"What does that mean?"

"It means that you don't have horseshit on your hands and you smell like a damned flower instead of a horse. Young fella, if you're a horse trader, then I'll kiss your sweet-smelling potootie!"

Dudley was shocked. "Well—" he stammered, "I *am* a horse trader."

"Oh yeah, then follow me to the corral around back and let's see if you know beans about horses."

Dudley saw no choice but to follow the filthy old coot. They trudged around the barn, a cavernous and rickety place, then stopped at a corral where four horses stood watching them with sudden interest.

"All right," Salty declared. "You tell me which is the best horse in that lot and which is the worst."

It would have been easy to refuse the challenge and just walk away but that wasn't Dudley's style. And besides, his uncle had taught him to judge horseflesh and he figured that it was no different here than it had been in Massachusetts. "Okay. I'll do it. Have you got a saddle and bridle?"

"What for?"

"If I'm to judge those animals, I want to put a bit between their teeth and ride them around the corral a few times. How else could a man really judge a saddle horse?"

"I could do it from right here," Salty declared. "But I won't."

"And I won't either," Dudley said, sticking his jaw out with determination. "And before I do judge them, I want a price."

"Some of 'em are worth considerably more than the others."

"Well give me an *average* price and, if it sounds fair, I'll buy a least three of the four, providing they aren't wild, dangerous, or unsound."

"There's no cripples or outlaws in that corral. They're all broken to saddle and I'll sell 'em for fifty dollars each, providing you take at least three."

Dudley didn't know if that was a good price out in Nevada, but he did know it would have been a steal back in Boston, where even average saddle horses sold for one hundred dollars.

"Very well," he decided, sticking out his hand. "Let's shake on that deal."

The old man grinned, squinting out from under a pair of bushy silver brows. "There's a saddle on a rack just inside the barn. You'll find a bridle and blanket draped over it."

Dudley quickly found the saddle and tossed it over the top pole of the corral. He took the bridle and reins, then entered the corral. The four horses moved nervously toward the back of the corral, eyeballing him suspiciously.

"Easy," he said, in the same gentle, relaxed voice that his uncle had taught him to use around livestock. "We're just going to take it easy today."

"Hell," Salty spat, "you sound like you're about to go to sleep with them four animals."

"Just let me do this my way," Dudley told the man quietly. "And maybe you'd like to go do something else until I'm finished in here."

"I wouldn't miss this for the world," Salty admitted.

"Then keep quiet and let me do this my way."

Salty spat tobacco, leaned on the fence, and grinned.

Dudley decided to try the buckskin first. It was a big, stout gelding with some white spots on its withers, indicating prior saddle sores. This was not necessarily a blemish or mark against the buckskin because many an animal had suffered from the inconsideration of its rider.

The buckskin allowed him to come up close and Dudley scratched the animal's ears, then slipped the bit into its mouth and over its head. He then checked the animal's teeth. "Smooth mouth. This horse is probably about twelve years old."

Salty didn't say a word, not even when Dudley saddled then mounted the gelding before riding it around and around the corral at a walk, then a trot.

"Horse is sound and willing," Dudley said, dismounting. "He's a good buy for someone who doesn't need a hardworking animal or one that is fast."

"You got that one pretty good," Salty had to admit.

"What next?"

"The sorrel mare."

"Have at 'er," Salty offered.

The sorrel was the best looking of the four horses, but when Dudley tried to approach her, she laid back her ears, spun around, and sent her heels flying at his head.

"Whoa!" Dudley said, barely dodging the mare's flying hooves. He turned to see Salty trying not to laugh. "That wasn't funny, dammit! That mare is an outlaw and you told me—"

"She can be ridden," Salty interrupted. "But only by a bronc buster and damn sure not by a dude like yourself. But I'll sell her to some cowboy who likes a flashy looking horse."

"Not to me you won't."

"That's right. You're no cowboy." Salty spit tobacco juice. "Okay, which horse is next?"

"The bay gelding."

Dudley caught the bay easy enough, then saddled and rode the animal. "Rough gaited. This one would pound your butt flat in no time," he called to the livery man.

65

"But he's sound and willing enough. Kind of lazy, though."

"He'll make a good farmer's horse. I've been told he pulls a plow or a wagon," Salty said. "That makes him worth fifty dollars easy."

Dudley supposed this was true. Back east, carriage horses were prized and worth considerable money, but this animal was no carriage horse and he wasn't very good looking. His head was too large and his neck too thin. Still, Dudley liked the homely fellow and figured he could be sold for at least fifty bucks.

"Last but not least," he said, studying the best prospect of the bunch, a black gelding with a white blaze and four white stockings. The black was tall, nearly sixteen hands with straight legs and an intelligent eye, as well as a good conformation.

But just as Dudley was about to approach the animal, Salty hollered, "hold up there young fella!"

"What?"

"That horse is no good and I don't want you to climb on his back."

"Why not?"

"He's a bad bucker." Salty shook his head. "Now I know he *looks* like a good one . . . but he's not."

"Thanks for the warning," Dudley replied, "but I'll try him out anyway."

"Naw," Salty argued. "You showed me that you do know a thing or two about judging animals so we can stop right here. I won't let you ride that black because you could get your neck broken and then I'd probably feel guilty and be responsible for getting you buried."

"Your concern is touching, but we agreed that I could buy three of the four and since the sorrel mare is vicious, that means I have to buy this one."

"Ah, never mind that," Salty said good naturedly. "I won't hold you to that deal."

"That doesn't matter because I'll hold *you* to it," Dudley told the man because he was on to his devious game. Salty didn't want him to ride the black because it was the best of the bunch and certainly worth more than fifty dollars.

"Easy," he said, reaching out for the animal and wondering if he might be wrong. But the black stood still and was soon saddled and bridled. All the while Dudley was getting the horse ready to ride, Salty kept telling what a bad bucker it was and how he'd sure get tossed and hurt.

"You're a real foolish young man," Salty finally said when Dudley shoved his toe into the stirrup, tensed, and then swung up on the animal's back. "You better get off quick 'cause that sonofagun is ready to explode!"

But Dudley held firm and waited, testing his theory. And sure enough, the black gelding didn't do a damned thing. After about a minute, Dudley nudged it with his heels and the horse moved forward just as easy as could be.

"He's got an easy gait to him," Dudley said as he passed the livery man the second time. "Like riding in the seat of a buggy."

"Oh yeah, but he's a sneaky bucker. Sometimes he is good but most generally not. What he's a'doin' is trying to lull you into thinking he's safe to ride. Any second now he's going to fly higher than a kite and you're going to find yourself draped over the top rail of this corral."

"I can wait," Dudley said, nudging the horse into a trot. "I sure do like this fine horse. Think I'll call him Midnight and he'll be the one that I keep for myself."

"You're a fool if you don't pay me any mind!"

Dudley chuckled out loud and brought the horse to a standstill. He dismounted, then ran his fingers carefully down the horse's legs, checking to make sure that he was completely sound and had not been foundered or cut. The legs were perfect and so were the black's hooves. Not a crack or a split . . . not a blemish on the entire animal.

"All right then," Dudley said, pulling out his traveling money and counting off one hundred and fifty dollars. "I'll take Midnight here and the bay and the buckskin."

"Dammit!" Salty swore. "You're making a terrible mistake. I don't think I can sell this black to you in good conscience."

Dudley's voice took on an edge. "Mister, we shook hands and I was told that, between *honorable* men, a handshake was as good as a signed contract. Now, are you an honorable man or a dishonest man?"

"Aw, all right! I'll take your money."

"And I'll want a bill of sale when I pick them up."

"It'll cost you four bits a day board. Do you have a saddle, bridle, halter, and blanket?"

"Nope."

"How about taking that saddle, bridle, and the other things you'll need and adding another fifty cash?"

"That is agreeable, but I'm out of cash. However, I have some funds coming in by telegraph in the next day or two. When it arrives, I'll pay you the boarding bill and the fifty for the tack. Fair enough?"

"Fair enough," Salty groused "But you skinned me pretty good."

Dudley laughed. "Isn't that what a horse trader is *supposed* to do?"

It was Salty's turn to laugh and then he said, "I underestimated you, young fella. You look and smell like a dandy but you damn sure do know horses and how to buy 'em right. That black is easy worth a hundred and I've had eighty offered for him already."

"Well," Dudley said, "I'm probably paying a little too much for the other pair so I doubt you've come out of this deal badly."

"I'll oil up your saddle and bridle real good for two dollars."

"Thanks." Dudley turned and started to leave. "Oh, and replace the latigo and the cinch. Don't want to have them break out on the trail someplace and spill me. Right?"

"Right," Salty reluctantly agreed, then grumbled under his breath, "damn it, I finally got stung . . . and by a greenhorn kid no less!"

Longarm was waiting for him in the lobby of the Washoe Hotel early that evening and they made a clumsy and not very convincing act of meeting by accident, then agreeing to go to dinner together.

When they were seated in a booth they picked for privacy, Longarm asked, "Well, did you find out anything?"

"No," Dudley admitted, "but I did buy three horses."

"That's good."

"What about you?"

Longarm told the kid everything that he had learned from Marshal Benson and ended by saying, "But they don't know for sure if the corrective shoe belongs to the murderer's horse."

"Well, at least we can be watching for the hoofprint of such an animal, can't we?"

"Yeah," Longarm said. "But there are thousands of horses in this area and the odds of seeing that print are slim. And even if we do, that isn't evidence that its owner is our man."

"I know, but it is something."

"You're right." Longarm took a sip of beer. He was hungry and wished that his steak would hurry up and arrive. "I'm going to find a wagon tomorrow and get it painted up like a medicine wagon. I'll stock it and leave Reno to start traveling around and asking questions."

"You'll need a horse to pull the wagon and I bought a steady bay gelding today at the Dollar Livery. He's yours to borrow."

"Thanks," Longarm said with appreciation.

"Think nothing of it. My uncle is sending me some traveling cash and, if you run low, just ask and you've got what you need. That's what a partner is supposed to do, isn't it?"

"Yeah," Longarm replied, feeling a bit embarrassed because it would never have occurred to him to offer a loan to Dudley Applewhite.

Their steaks arrived and they both ate ravenously, although Dudley had better table manners. After they were finished, the young deputy marshal said, "Well, what now?"

"Let's split up and go saloon hopping," Longarm said. "We can bump into each other here for breakfast and compare notes."

"Sounds good."

"Just remember not to seem real nosy or people will get suspicious," Longarm advised. "Casually bring up the subject of the murders, then let it rest and see if anyone has any comments."

"I got it. Does anyone in town know who we are?"

"Yeah, a few." Longarm told his friend about how Marshal Ralph Benson had spilled the beans and told several of his friends as well as family.

"That's a shame," Dudley said. "Will it make things harder?"

"Probably. The word will get out but there's nothing we can do about it. I'm hoping that when we head out of town the word will stay here in Reno and we'll be fine."

"Can we at least sort of keep in the same general vicinity?"

"I don't know," Longarm said. "I told you we need to operate independently and that I plan to start up on the Comstock Lode."

"I've heard of that place and I can't wait to see it."

Longarm frowned and then relented. "All right. You follow along a few miles and we'll meet up there at . . .

oh, the Bucket of Blood Saloon in three days."

"Hell of name," Dudley said.

"Hell of a town," Longarm replied as he got up and left the kid from Boston.

Chapter 7

Longarm had always enjoyed going around to the various saloons. They were the center of a frontierman's world, and, for the price of a beer or two, you could quickly measure the pulse of a town. You could hear all the local gossip and learn right away if the town was a good place to live and work. Every town had its own flavor or pulse, so to speak. Mining towns, for example, were peopled by restless, get-rich-quick men who lived hard and generally died hard. There was usually an air of desperation in mining towns and everyone was either going to get rich tomorrow or else they'd already gotten rich and lost all their newfound wealth to cards, women, or liquor and generally to an overdose of all three.

Cattle towns were more permanent and so were those dependent on farming or timber. Reno was such a town. Much of its prosperity did come down from the famed Comstock Lode, but there was also an air of permanence about Reno and a whole lot less fussing and fighting. Most people in this town figured that, long after Virginia City and Silver City had gone bust and its hard rock miners were gone, Reno would continue to grow in its own leisurely pace, thanks to its mixed economy and the railroad, which formed a solid employment base.

Along Virginia Street there were many familiar and inviting saloons. And this evening the air was cool and invigorating. Longarm swore he could almost smell pines from the nearby Sierras. The first saloon he ducked into for a beer and to catch the local gossip was called the Waterhole, which had always been a good source of gossip. It was a fairly typical saloon with sawdust on the floor, a long, polished bar, and some tables for men who wanted to play cards or just rest their feet after a long day on the job. It also had a brass foot rail for you to rest a boot upon.

"I'll have a beer and one of your best cigars," Longarm told the bartender as he laid his money down and smiled at the other patrons lined up for their libations.

"Comin' right up!" the bartender, a small man with red hair and even redder suspenders shouted.

Longarm watched him select a cigar from a big glass jar and then grab a bottle of beer. "Welcome to the Waterhole. You look familiar. Have you been here before?"

"Once or twice."

"My name is Ed," the bartender told him. "You need refills, you just shout and I'll be along. The beer is two bits, the cigar is the same."

Longarm paid him and then he licked the cigar and bit off its tip. The tobacco was dark and he had a hunch that it was strong and from Mexico. No matter, he'd enjoy it all the same.

Right beside him, two men in city clothes were discussing local politics and Longarm twisted around to face the door, hooked a heel over the foot rail, and listened as he struck a match. The cigar was even stronger than expected and it bit at his nostrils.

"That sonofabitch smells like smokin' dog shit!" a mule skinner shouted. "Holy smokin' hell! You oughta throw that sonofabitch in the spittoon and roll yourself a cigarette!"

Longarm shrugged. "It's strong," he agreed, "but I like the taste."

"Then your taste ain't fer shit!"

Longarm turned back to the bar. He would try to ignore the mule skinner who had obviously had too much to drink. The pair next to him had stopped their conversation when Longarm had lit his cigar, but now they resumed talking. Longarm heard the cowboy mutter some further insults but he paid them no mind.

On his left side, a second pair were discussing the case of a man who had killed another in a knife fight and was now being transported to prison in Carson City.

"I think Homer got what he deserved," one said. "After all, that bastard was fooling around with Ernie's wife."

"Yeah, but she fooled around with lots of men, so it didn't matter."

"It mattered to Ernie. You see, maybe his wife was unfaithful more often than no . . . but at least she kept it a secret. Now Homer was just braggin' to everyone he met about how he was humpin' Ernie's wife. I ask you straight out . . . how could a man stand that kind of insult?"

"I don't know. I think that Ernie should have divorced his wife. After all, he owns a good business, and even if he does stink 'cause he never bathes, his wife is no prize."

"You're right. She's ugly and she's ornery. But Ernie loves the woman and they do have a son who's barely out of diapers."

"Yeah, I know. Ugly little bastard. Crying his head off every time I've seen him. Maybe that kid was the thing that drove Ernie's wife into ruin."

"Who could say? There's a lot we don't know about what goes on in this town. I'm beginning to think that none of the murders will ever be solved. That last one sorta made my flesh crawl."

"Yeah, mine, too. You hate to see a man's throat slit open like he was a butchered hog. And you know that Marshal Benson ain't never going to figure out who is behind the killings and robberies. I tell you, I watch my back when I am out at night."

"Well, several of the killings took place in broad daylight."

"Yeah, but they were always out from town."

"Might not be the next time, though."

"You're right about that."

Longarm turned to the pair and said, "I just arrived on the train from Cheyenne. What's this about murders and robberies?"

The shorter of the two men drained his beer and placed it on the bar calling, "Hey, Ed! How about a refill!"

"Be right along," the bartender shouted.

The man with the empty beer glass looked up at Longarm. "You mean to say that you haven't heard about the killings that have been taking place in these parts?"

"No," Longarm lied. "How many have there been?"

"At least a dozen." The man looked at his companion, who nodded somberly and added, "I'd be willing to bet that . . . for every one that we know about . . . two have taken place that we aren't even aware of. I'm saying that there might be twenty or thirty dead that just disappeared."

Longarm feigned shock. "You're kidding!"

"No, sir! Someone in these parts is killing and robbing on a grand scale. This whole town is spooked right now. And I've heard that the people out on the homesteads and ranches are really nervous."

"They should be," the other man said. "I wouldn't want to be some solitary miner, rancher, or farmer."

"Well," Longarm asked, "what's being done about this outbreak of murders and robberies?"

"Not much."

"I find that hard to believe."

"You had better believe it. We have a marshal that don't want to do his job. I think he's even scared of getting killed if he starts going out of town and poking around too much."

Longarm motioned for Ed to bring three beers on his tab. When they all had fresh ones, he said, "I can't believe that so many are being killed and nothing is being done to catch the murderer."

The taller man shrugged. "In fairness to Marshal Benson, where would he even begin to start looking? I mean, the killings are happening all over the place. Some on the Comstock Lode, some north of town. Why, there was even a Paiute named Indian Charlie got his throat cut. It was rumored that he had some gold, and when they found his body, he'd been tortured before being killed."

Longarm shook his head. "I might be moving out of these parts."

"What are you here for, stranger?"

"I'm dispensing medicine from a wagon. Only I haven't bought the wagon yet."

"You're a snake oil peddler?" the belligerent mule skinner bellowed. "That's what you are? A gawdamn flim-flam medicine man!"

Longarm smiled, hoping that the drunken mule skinner would go back to his own ruminations. But that wasn't to be. The man pushed off from the bar, then shoved one of the city men aside to stand toe to toe with Longarm. He had close-set eyes that radiated pure meanness. His nose had been busted in many a brawl, and he was big and strong and just as smelly as his mules. Longarm had a feeling that he frequently got drunk and then loved to brawl and nothing pleased him more than whipping a big stranger.

The mule skinner stabbed a finger into Longarm's chest and said, "I hate your kind of fella. You don't do nothin' but take sick people's money and then give 'em some poison. You're worse than a gawdamn parasite. You're nothin' but stinkin' dog shit vermin."

"Why don't you get lost," Longarm said quietly. "Otherwise, I'll have to hurt you."

"You and what army!"

Longarm could have driven his fist into the man's solar plexus. He had a big head and heavy jaw that told Longarm that his skull was as thick as that of a horse and one that an opponent could bust his knuckles against. Longarm also knew that the mule skinner would be a hard man to put down for keeps. Even drunk, he'd be cunning and vicious. You would get hurt some beating this man into submission.

"Hey," the bartender shouted, hurrying toward them. "Bert, you leave that man alone."

"I don't like him."

The bartender looked at Longarm, apology written all over his round, sweaty face. "Stranger, you'd best leave. I can't—"

The man's words died on his lips as Longarm blew a cloud of smelly smoke into the mule skinner's ugly face, then drew his gun in a lightning quick move, and then slammed its heavy barrel against Bert's thick skull. The mule skinner rocked backward, bounced off the heavy bar, and started to raise his fists when Longarm busted him a second time over his right ear. Bert's legs buckled and he reached out to support himself on the bar with one hand while reaching for either a gun or a knife with the other hand. Longarm pistol-whipped him a third time right across the forehead, opening a deep gash and Bert's eyes rolled up in his head.

"Holy smokes!" one of the townsmen shouted as blood gushed down Bert's brutish face as the man sagged against the bar. "You really hit him hard."

Longarm reached down and grabbed the mule skinner by one limp but very muscular arm. The man was conscious, but just barely. Custis dragged him through the dirty sawdust and out across the boardwalk and dumped him in the street.

He washed his hands in a horse watering trough and went back inside the saloon, passing Dudley whose presence he had not noticed.

"Damn, Custis, you like to killed that man!" the Boston kid swore. "Did you have to hit him *three* times?"

"Twice didn't seem to do the job," Longarm hissed as he passed the young marshal. "And I wasn't about to bust up my fists on such worthless trash."

He returned to the bar still puffing his cigar. "Now, as you were saying about those murders?"

"Man," one of the city fellas swore in amazement. "Do you drink your own medicine?"

"A bottle a day," Longarm said straight-faced.

"I think I'm going to want to buy a case judging on what you did to Bert. I seen him whip men and once I even seen him lose . . . though the winner was also beaten half to death. But I never saw anyone take care of him so fast and so completely."

Longarm just shrugged. "With a man like that, you hit him quick and hard and as often as required and preferably with a club or the barrel of your pistol. If I'd have punched that man, I'd have broken my knuckles and then he'd have had the advantage."

"You're right! I've seen Bert whip men who broke their hands on his skull."

"Not me," Longarm said.

"You'd have been better off to kill him," the bartender said, looking worriedly toward the front door. "Bert will remember what you did and he'll be hunting for you every night."

"If he finds me," Longarm warned, "he'll be in even sorrier shape than he is right now."

Everyone heard Longarm say that and no one looked as if they doubted his words.

A few minutes later, Longarm finished his beer and headed for the door calling, "I'll see you gents another time."

Men nodded or waved and when they were sure that Longarm was gone, they went outside to stare at Bert still lying unconscious in the street.

"Never thought I'd see the day someone would whip him so quick and easy," a man said.

"Me neither. Hope the big snake oil peddler has eyes in the back of his head or Bert will kill him for sure."

"I dunno," another man remarked. "I seen that big fella before, and it seems to me he was a United States Marshal."

"Naw!"

"Seems to me he was," the man persisted.

"I hope he was," someone said. " 'Cause, if he's really a lawman, it might mean that he's here to catch whoever has been murdering and robbing everyone."

"Yeah," another man said. "Let's go back inside and toast the big stranger and hope he broke Bert's head and left him a droolin' idiot who can't hurt anyone anymore."

The crowd of patrons of the Waterhole Saloon stomped back inside and ordered another round. Meanwhile, Marshal Dudley Applewhite sat quietly in a corner wondering at the sudden and devastating savagery of the man called Longarm.

Chapter 8

Longarm felt mighty good sleeping in a solid bed that night. In the morning, he had a big breakfast then headed off to the town's liveries, hoping to find a wagon that he could paint and live in while he traveled about selling medicine and whatever other cheap wares that he could afford to stock.

The Dollar Livery was first on his mental list of places to visit and remembered that this was where young Dudley had bought three horses, one of which he had offered to Longarm to use as a combination saddle horse and wagon puller. That had been very generous, reinforcing Longarm's suspicion that the kid came from a wealthy background. Nothing wrong with that, except those kind often folded up their tent and went packing when the going got tough.

"Howdy!" Longarm called in greeting to a dirty old gent in a pair of coveralls. "I understand that a young man named Dudley bought some horses from you yesterday."

The old livery man nodded. "What's it to you?"

"Well, he offered to let me take one of them."

"You'd have to talk to him about that."

"I know," Longarm said. "He said it was a bay."

81

"Yeah, the ugly one that he bought from me."

"Mind if I see the animal?"

"Course not. He's in the corral out back."

"I also need a medicine wagon," Longarm said, looking around at several wagons in various states of repair. "You have any idea where I might find one for sale or rent?"

"What the devil would you want with a medicine wagon?"

"I want to heal the sick and give hope to the afflicted," Longarm deadpanned.

"Oh, horse manure." Salty Bates eyed Longarm suspiciously. "You ain't no travelin' peddler. What's your game, mister? I got a hunch you and that young dandy are up to something fishy."

"Nope," Longarm told him, starting around the barn.

Salty fell in behind Longarm and when they reached the corral, the older man said, "That's the one."

Longarm sighed. "That's the ugliest horse I've seen in a long, long time. You really got to young Dudley, didn't you."

"The hell I did!" Salty swore, spitting a torrent of tobacco juice into the dirt between them. "That young fella is the one that got to me! You see that black gelding and the buckskin?"

"Yeah. Well, he bought them two and the bay for fifty dollars each."

"The bay isn't worth fifty dollars," Longarm said, "but the other two look to be pretty fair horses."

"They are! They're both worth more'n I sold 'em to the kid for. And that bay that you think is so ugly . . . well, he's sound and he's got heart. And I'll tell you something you'd never guess . . . that ugly sonofabitch can run like the wind."

"No!"

"It's true," Salty insisted. "I bought him from a fella

that won some money racing him. Of the four horses, he's probably the fastest."

Longarm had to grin. "If he's fast, it's because he's so ugly he's had to run from the other horses all his life."

"Might be true," Salty conceded. "Anyway, I was told that he'll pull a wagon."

Longarm frowned. "Do you have any idea where I can find a wagon to paint up and use to sell medicine out the back?"

"As a matter of fact, I do."

Longarm blinked with surprise. "Where?"

"Well," Salty said, "I'm not exactly sure if the wagon is for sale or not, but I do know that the man who owns it is in a lot of trouble."

"Law trouble?"

"No, he drank up his medicine and got real drunk, then he gambled away his horse. He's parked a few blocks up the street in the poor part of town. Last I heard, he was sweeping out saloons and trying to save up enough money to buy another wagon horse and some snake oil mixins."

"What's his name?"

"Gilroy. Otis Gilroy." Salty clucked his tongue. "When he's sober and cleaned up, he can sell most anything at twice what it is worth. He's smooth when he's workin', but right now he's in sorry, sorry shape."

"What's a wagon like his worth?"

Salty stuck out his hand. "I don't give free advice, mister. Cost you five dollars."

"Never mind. I can find out myself."

"Be worth it to you if I came along and sort of greased the skids. Gilroy can be ornery and stubborn as a Missouri mule."

Longarm considered these words. "Tell you what. If you strike a deal that I approve of for the man's wagon, I'll pay you five dollars. If not, I'll pay you two dollars for your time and effort."

"Fair enough," Salty readily agreed. "I like Gilroy, but the man is in the wrong line of business riding around selling snake oil and havin' fun with the farmers' wives and daughters. He's been shot twice by jealous husbands and fathers and beat to a pulp more times than I remember."

"Well," Longarm said, "I have no intention of dallying with anyone's wife or daughter."

"Sure," Salty remarked with a wink. "You just want to ride around and peddle snake oil 'cause it makes you feel good to help folks."

"That's right."

"In a pig's eye!" Salty said with a laugh.

Longarm didn't much care if the old reprobate believed him or not. But if the man could help him purchase a wagon already outfitted as a medicine wagon, then he'd be well worth his wage.

Ten minutes later, they rounded a corner and there was the medicine wagon. It was painted bright red with big letters that proclaimed, OTIS GILROY, PHYSICIAN OF HEALTH, M.D. & T.P.

"What," Longarm asked, "does T.P. stand for?"

"Tooth puller. Otis is better pulling teeth than he is at the medicine part." Salty grinned and showed his own missing teeth. "He's pulled three of mine. 'Course, he insists that you drink a bottle of his painkiller first."

"Is it tasty?"

"As a matter of fact it is," Salty replied, licking his lips. "I don't know what Otis puts into the bottles besides bad liquor, but whatever it is tastes special, although it will near always give you the next-day trots."

As they approached the medicine wagon, Longarm studied it carefully. He was certainly not an expert on wagons and this one looked as if it had traveled many a hard mile. Its red paint was peeling and there were places where tin cans had been nailed over holes in the sides of the wagon bed. This was obviously a converted Conestoga wagon, the kind that the pioneers had used to cross the Great Plains. But Gilroy or someone else had replaced the top canvas with a wooden box covered with a high tin roof. A blackened smokestack poked out the top and Longarm could not imagine how the wagon would fare in a high, broadside wind.

Still, none of its wheel spokes were missing and all the parts seemed to fit. "It sure is ugly."

"It'll go with that bay horse," Salty remarked. "Be unkind to hitch a handsome animal to such a homely wagon."

"Will it make it up to the the Comstock Lode?"

"Sure! I had it worked on last month for Otis. A wheelwright tightened the rims and made sure that everything is working fine. It's a little on the heavy side, but that bay ought to be able to pull it up to Virginia City if you give him plenty of breathers."

"What is it worth?"

"I wouldn't give him more than a hundred dollars for it and everything inside."

"Hmmm," Longarm mused. "I wouldn't have thought it would be worth even that much."

"Maybe you could rent it from Otis for a while," Salty suggested.

"That's a pretty good idea," Longarm said. "Do you think he is inside?"

"I expect so. I never knew Otis Gilroy to go to bed before dawn nor get up before noon. And he's most always bedded down with some floozy."

Longarm walked up to the back door and stepped up on a ladder. He knocked. "Mr. Gilroy?"

He heard a grunt. "Mr. Gilroy?"

"Get lost!"

Longarm looked over his shoulder at Salty. "Well?"

"Open the damned door and make him get up."

Longarm grabbed the door handle and gave it a yank. The door was latched from the inside but so flimsy that it nearly pulled out of its hinges. "Hey!" Longarm called. "We need to talk."

In reply, he heard the sound of a gun being cocked. Longarm jumped off the steps just as a bullet smashed through the door. It would have hit him for certain had he not moved.

"Who the hell is out there!" Gilroy bellowed.

"It's me and a customer!" Salty shouted. "Open up. We got business to discuss."

They both heard some cussing not only from Gilroy, but from a woman. After several minutes, the door bounced open and Longarm beheld a tall man in red flannel underwear. He had a long, unshaven face and wild silver and black hair. At one time, he would have been handsome, but not anymore. Age and hard living had driven deep lines into his face and now he had a prominent pot belly, which protruded from the underwear because of missing buttons.

"Salty, you know better'n to wake me up so early!"

"Shoot the old dog!" the woman inside cried. "Just blow his old guts out for wakin' us so early."

"Who is it this time?" Salty asked.

"I don't know. One of the gals at the Depot Saloon. Forget her name. Maybe she never told me, but she's a wildcat in the sack." Gilroy gave Longarm a hard stare. "You the one that was bangin' on my door then nearly tore it loose?"

"That's right."

"He wants to buy your wagon," Salty interrupted. "He'll pay you a fair price."

"She ain't for sale!"

"Then he'll *rent* the wagon if you provide him with some snake oil to peddle."

Gilroy belched. Then, he nearly fell off his little porch

trying to climb down the stairs, after which he opened his flannels and peed on his rear wheel. Finished with his business, he farted, scratched, then turned around with his flaccid tool still exposed and said, "Now what the hell do you want to sell snake oil for, mister?"

Longarm had no good answer. Especially with Gilroy standing before him exposed and revealed. "I . . ."

"How much money do you got?" Gilroy asked.

"Enough."

"You need to get out of town and trick someone or something?"

"Sort of."

"Ha!" Gilroy cried. "Now I begin to understand."

Longarm very much doubted that fact but said nothing.

"I won't sell this beauty," Gilroy said, stifling a yawn. "It's my home, you see. I love it and I got no other."

"Then I'll rent it for a . . . month."

"Hmmm," Gilroy mused, looking down and tucking his limp rod into his flannels without looking the least bit embarrassed. "It would cost you five dollars a day and it don't come with no damned horse 'cause mine is dead."

"He's got a horse," Salty said. "And that is way too steep. I can sell him a wagon for that much."

"Well then do it!"

"Wait a minute," Longarm said. "I'll pay you one hundred dollars for one month, but only if you make up some of your snake oil for me to peddle."

"I could do that. I'll sell it to you for . . . a dollar a bottle. Anything you get over that is pure profit."

"Hellfire!" Salty cried. "That's what you sell it for to the public!"

Gilroy's eyes squinted. "You always did have a big mouth, Salty. One of these days I'm gonna slam it shut for keeps!"

"Any time you want to try!" the smaller man said, raising his fists.

87

Longarm had heard enough. "Wait a minute! I've heard enough. Now Mr. Gilroy, if you want to do business, then I'll expect you to clean everything up inside and have me fifty bottles of your patent medicine ready to sell."

"I can do that in . . . oh, about a week."

"By tomorrow."

"Geezus, man! You have no idea how hard it is to brew the secret formula that will cure the sick and heal the lame and—"

"Aw shut up," Salty ordered. "Just do the job and take the man's money. In a month, you can have enough of a stake to go back out on the road with a live horse that will sell you."

Gilroy's face twisted with contempt. "I wouldn't buy another horse from you if you was the last man in Nevada! You're the one that sold me the horse that died!"

"That's because you got drunk and poured a bad batch of the formula down his gullet!"

Longarm shook his head. "I'll give you one hundred twenty-five dollars when I pick up the wagon tomorrow morning along with fifty bottles of snake oil . . . if you've cleaned and aired out that wagon."

"Take it, you lame-headed fool!" the woman inside screeched. "Where else you gonna get that kind of money?"

"But I ain't got no money to buy the formula!"

Longarm reached into his pants and withdrew ten dollars. "This ought to do it."

Gilroy's fingers plucked the money away with practiced ease. He smacked his lips and said, "Might take a little more than this, mister."

"You'll get it when I pick up the wagon tomorrow morning at eight. If it isn't spotless and that woman isn't gone and if you get drunk on that money, I'll whip you up one side and down the other. In short, Mr. Gilroy, I'll make you wish you'd never been born."

The man swallowed hard. He looked over at Salty, who said, "I'll help you get things in order. I've got a bay that is going to pull this wagon. I'll bring him over and drag this rolling shit house over to my barn and we'll get her ready for tomorrow."

"Thanks," Gilroy muttered, looking down at his feet.

"Don't thank me," Salty told him. "I'm only doing it so that I can get rid of that ugly bay horse."

But Longarm knew better. This pair was rough and profane, but he sensed they were good and longtime friends. Otis Gilroy had fallen on hard times and maybe part of it was that Salty had sold him a sick horse. At any rate, he was pretty sure that the two old reprobates would have him a medicine wagon by tomorrow morning.

Chapter 9

Dudley met Longarm in the hotel lobby that evening and, while pretending to read the local paper, they quietly exchanged what news they had gathered. Longarm told him about renting a medicine wagon and getting Otis Gilroy to bottle up some snake oil.

"Then I guess you'll be on your way," Dudley said.

"I'm leaving for the Comstock Lode in the morning. I'll be hitching that ugly bay horse to the wagon."

"What will you use for a saddle if you have to leave the wagon and head out in hurry?"

"I hadn't thought of that but I guess I ought to buy a saddle, bridle, and blanket from Salty."

"I'd think so," Dudley replied. "Have you learned anything more about the case?"

"No." Longarm turned a page. "We are starting on a cold trail. There hasn't been a murder and robbery in several weeks."

"What if our man just up and left this area? How will we know?"

"If he left, we'll try to find out who he was and where he went," Longarm told the younger man. "And, if we can't at least do that, then we'll get back on the train and return to Denver."

"I'd hate to go back empty-handed."

"Me, too. But sometimes, you come up empty no matter how hard you try. And don't forget, there is always the possibility that our man could die a violent death. It happens often enough out west."

"You're saying that our murderer could be knifed or mugged and we'd never know it."

"That's right." Longarm frowned. "I've been on cases where the killer just vanished. When that happened, I told myself that he either got scared and changed his ways—although that is not real likely because killers enjoy killing too much to stop—or else they were themselves killed."

"I see what you mean."

"Listen," Longarm said. "Why don't we meet at the Dollar Livery tomorrow about ten o'clock when I hope to pull out? We can sort of make our plans and go from there."

"All right. But what about this evening?"

"Try the saloons again."

"If I were you, I wouldn't try the Waterhole. That Bert fella looks like the kind who won't let bygones be by-gones."

"You're right and I'll keep a sharp eye out for him."

Longarm stood up to leave. "There's a saloon called the Frontier. That's where I'll be at least during the early part of the evening. You might want to go back to the Waterhole."

"All right," Dudley agreed. "See you in the morning."

"Right. Oh, did you get that money you had sent from home?"

"I did," he said, patting the inside pocket of his coat. "It's right here."

"You shouldn't carry so much cash. It invites trouble."

"You're probably right. I'll deposit most of it tomorrow morning."

"Just be careful," Longarm warned. "If you have any trouble, you know where I can be found."

Dudley watched Longarm get up, fold the free hotel newspaper, and saunter outside. He picked up the paper and read for a few minutes, then followed Longarm's example and headed back to the Waterhole. Dudley had never been one to spend much time in eastern bars or saloons. It just hadn't been his style. But no sooner had he ordered a beer than one of the younger and prettier saloon ladies came over to join him. She was short and buxom with curly brown hair. She reminded Dudley of an old flame and when she asked him to buy her a drink, he was more than happy to do so.

"So you're new to town, aren't you," the girl said after introducing herself as Marlene.

"I am."

"Someone as tall and handsome as yourself definitely stands out in this crowd."

He felt his cheeks warm. "Thanks. If you don't mind me saying so, you also stand out from the others."

Marlene smiled and touched his arm. "You're a flatterer and I can tell from your accent that you come from back east. I'd guess Boston."

"And you'd be correct. Where are you from?"

"Philadelphia. I've only been in Nevada a year."

"Why did you leave the East?"

She shrugged. "We all have skeletons in our past. Sometimes, the best thing to do is to leave them far behind. Let's just say that I was sort of what you might call the black sheep of my family. My father was a very strict man. He'd quote us kids the Bible and he never thought of sparing the rod. I ran away as soon as I met a man that I thought would take good care of me."

93

Dudley leaned closer. "And does he still 'take care of you'?"

"No. When we got up to the Comstock, I found out that he expected me to take care of him! Can you imagine?"

"No, I can't."

"Well," Marlene said, "he did. And when I refused to do what he wanted me to do with other men for money, he busted me in the face so hard he broke my nose. Can you see how it is knocked a little to this side?"

She touched her nose with her finger and he nodded. "If you hadn't mentioned it, I wouldn't have noticed."

"You're sweet to say that." Marlene shrugged. "Anyway, I knew I had to get away from the man, but when I came back to Reno I didn't have the fare to go to another town. I had been thinking of California, but the fare was twenty dollars and I was dead broke. And you know what happens to young women when they are broke."

"I suppose bad things happen."

"Exactly!" She took a drink and her eyes met her reflection in the bar mirror. "I was offered plenty of jobs—all requiring the prone position, if you know what I mean. But I knew what happened to those girls and I wanted no part of it. Then I met the owner of this saloon and he asked me if I could sing and dance."

"And of course you could."

Marlene giggled. "How did you guess! Well, actually, my voice isn't all that good and I'd never danced for the public. But I had seen Lotta Crabtree up on the Comstock, and when I saw the kind of money and success she was having, well, I figured I could do okay and I was right."

"So why didn't you go to California?"

"I'm going to San Francisco when I leave here. But for now, the owner and the bartenders all watch out for me and the customers know the score. And I make lots and lots of money."

The bartender arrived with a whiskey for Marlene and a refill of his beer. When he was gone, the young woman asked, "I've talked enough about myself. What's your line of business?"

He stared at the foamy head on his beer. "I'm . . . I'm a horse trader."

She stared and punched him lightly in the shoulder. "Aw, come on, Dudley! You're way too young."

He looked with amusement. "Then tell me, how old do you have to be?"

"Well, I don't know. How old are you?"

"Twenty-five," he lied. "How old are you?"

Marlene pursed her lips and gave the question some serious thought. "To be honest, some mornings I feel like I'm about forty. But I guess I'm really only about half that old, actually."

"So you're twenty?"

"Yep, but going on forty."

"Why do you say that? You're still young and very pretty. We've both got our whole lives ahead of us."

"Yeah, but that's the problem, isn't it?"

Dudley shook his head. "I don't understand."

Marlene wrinkled her nose and tossed down the rest of her whiskey. "Do you mind buying me a refill?"

"Of course not."

"Because, if you don't keep buying me drinks, I'm supposed to move on to another."

"Then I'll buy you drinks all evening."

She looked right into his eyes. "I was kinda hoping you'd say that. Now, what do you really do?"

He took her arm and led her over to a table, motioning for the bartender to bring them another round. Whiskey this time for them both because he was bloating up on the beer. Once they were seated, he leaned forward and whispered. "Marlene, can you keep a secret?"

"Sure. You can trust me."

Dudley reached into his pocket and dragged out his badge, holding it close so that no one else in the saloon could see its shine.

Marlene stared. "Oh my gosh, did you steal it from a lawman!"

"No, I *am* a lawman. A federal marshal."

"You're kidding!"

"Shhh." He put the badge away. "I'm working to capture whoever has been killing those farmers and people. You know, the one that has slit so many throats before robbing his victims."

"Yeah!" Her eyes widened. "There's a lot of talk around here about who is doing that. I've heard everything."

"I'm listening," he said. "But don't let on what we're talking about. You see, I'm working in secret. Undercover we call it. If the word was to get out that I was after the murder—or murderers—then my life could be in great danger."

"I understand completely." She looked around then leaned forward. "I'd like to talk about this, but not here. Too dangerous."

"Where then?"

"I have a room upstairs."

"Here in the saloon?"

"Yeah. They gave it to me cheap. If you want to learn what I know about them murders, then buy me another drink and when it's gone, we'll sort of mosey upstairs. Me first, and you can follow. Third door on the right."

"Okay." Dudley had actually lost track of the drinks and when he went over to get refills, he discovered he was a little unsteady on his feet and thought, I probably should have stayed with the beer. No matter. If I find out something important from Marlene, Longarm is finally going to be impressed.

When the bartender poured him two more rounds, Dudley leaned forward and whispered, "The lady and I are going upstairs . . . but only to talk."

He winked and the bartender shrugged.

Marlene had already disappeared upstairs so Dudley emptied both glasses as he waited for several minutes so that no one but the bartender would realize what was happening. It was about then that the foulmouthed mule skinner named Bert slammed in through the doorway with his head swathed in bandages. He looked like he was wearing a turban, which took all of Dudley's willpower not to start giggling.

He could hear the mule skinner's loud mouth but was not able to decipher his words over the general conversation. *Well, Deputy Marshal Applewhite, you've waited long enough. It's time to go upstairs and find out what Marlene knows. Hope it's good!*

Dudley got up from his chair and started for the stairs, but he accidentally hooked the toe of his shoe on a man's chair and crashed face first into the sawdust.

"Jeezus, mister," the man whose chair he'd bumped exclaimed. "Why don't you watch where you're walking!"

"Sorry," Dudley said, looking up and then climbing back to his feet. He brushed the sawdust off his clothes and accidentally dusted the men at the table, who didn't take that very well.

"What the hell is the matter with you, ya clumsy oaf!"

"Sorry," Dudley repeated.

"Well, sorry don't do it. Ya dusted all three of us and now we got sawdust in our beers to boot!"

"I'll buy you fresh ones."

"Ya better. Dumb dude."

Dudley finished brushing himself off then said, "I apologized and offered to buy you three . . . gentlemen . . . beers. I see no need for you to be offensive and insulting."

The closest man to him stood up and growled. "You're drunk, ya stupid jerk."

In reply, Dudley burped in the man's face, prompting him to throw a punch. Normally, Dudley would have ducked it easily and countered with a jolting uppercut to the man's midsection. But the beer and the whiskey betrayed him and he didn't quite manage to get out of the way of the roundhouse swing. Next thing he knew, he was slamming over another tableful of cussing men.

Things went downhill very quickly after that. Dudley tried to apologize to the second bunch of men, but one of them was crude and tried to knock him down again. This time, Dudley landed his own solid punch and the melee was on. Suddenly, everyone was fighting and Dudley found himself on the bottom of a big pile of dirty, profane, and very angry customers. They were clawing, kicking, gouging, and punching like a bag of wet wildcats and it took all of his strength to climb out from under the pile and finally reach the stairs.

Without looking back but hearing the sound of screams, breaking glass, and fists thudding against flesh, he crawled up the steps and reached the landing, his face numb and badly bruised, his clothes covered with sawdust and blood . . . much of which was his own.

He crawled up the stairs, dusted himself as well as he could, then staggered down the hallway to Marlene's door and knocked.

"Great gawd, what happened to you!"

He waved his hand and pushed inside. "Well, I tripped over a fella's chair, then he punched me and when I got up someone else wanted to fight and the next thing I knew everyone was brawling."

"Sit down! You look terrible!"

Dudley sank down on her bed. "I feel terrible, too."

"You need to be cleaned up. And your shirt and coat are all messed up."

"I'll need a new wardrobe, that's for sure." Dudley cradled his head in his hands. "I also need a doctor."

"No," she replied, "you just need a bath and some medication. I'll get some water and you can take one nice, hot soak."

"Here? In *your* room?"

"Why not?"

"But—"

"Don't be silly. I've seen plenty of naked men. I'm no shrinking violet and I haven't been a virgin in years. Now get undressed while I go down the hallway and bring back your bathwater."

Dudley was too tired and depressed to argue. He undressed and feeling quite tipsy, he stretched out on Marlene's soft bed and he must have dozed off quick because, the next thing he knew, she was rousing and then dragging him toward a tub of nice warm, fragrant bathwater.

"Just sit there and soak for a minute," she told him.

"I could use a drink."

"I think you've had enough for this evening."

"My head hurts."

"All right. I'll pour us a strong one."

Dudley was greatly relieved. He was not normally much of a drinking man and that was probably why he'd gotten in trouble downstairs. But right now he felt so awful that a little more whiskey could not possibly compound his discomfort.

When Marlene handed him a glass of whiskey, he looked up and his jaw dropped. "You're . . . naked!"

She shimmied and giggled. "That's right. This bathtub is big enough for two and I mean to take advantage of that fact. Scoot down to your end and I'll sit here at the other end. Come on, now!"

Dudley grinned but instantly regretted it as his split lip sent a stab of pain through his head. "Ouch!"

"Poor boy. You really look as if you were worked over pretty bad down there. Those men like to fight, you know.

They do it quite regularly. At least three or four times a week."

"Well doesn't the bartender try to stop them?"

"Not if he values his own hide." Marlene rolled forward onto her knees raising a bar of soap and a washcloth.

"Wait," he protested. "Couldn't we—"

"No. You have blood on your face, in your hair, and it has to be scrubbed off. Take a drink and don't whine about it."

"I'll try not to."

Marlene gently washed his face and then his hair. "You've got a pretty nasty gash in your scalp. What did someone hit you with, a beer bottle?"

"I don't know. I felt like I was being crushed by a mountain. The whole thing was like a bad dream. I was lucky to get out from under that pile alive."

She finished washing his face and then rinsed his hair. "Your poor face is going to be even more of a mess in the morning. One of your eyes is swelling shut and the other has a shiner. You've got a big bruise on your right cheekbone and one of your ears is all swollen. But I guess you ought to feel lucky it wasn't bitten completely off."

"They do that here?"

"Oh, sure! And you're much too handsome to have only one ear."

"Well, I wouldn't like that very much at all. Men don't bite off each other's ears in Boston."

"This isn't Boston. I've even seen men nip off their opponent's nose in a hard fight."

Dudley nearly swooned at the thought of losing his nose. "Doesn't anyone fight fair?"

"Honey, there is no such thing as a fair fight. Someone wins and someone loses. The best that can happen is that the one that wins doesn't make the one that loses hurt too bad or too long. I've seen eyes gouged out. Teeth busted out. Arms twisted nearly off. Ribs broken. Kneecaps shat-

tered and feet stomped so hard they looked like pan-
cakes."

"Is it that way all over the West?"

"I can't say," Marlene told him as she leaned forward,
firm breasts and large nipples just inches from his battered
face.

"Mind if I . . . well, kissed them?" he blurted without
thinking.

"What?"

He swallowed hard then pointed. "You know. Those."

"I thought you were in terrible pain. You *look* to be in
pain."

"I am in pain but . . . well, they sure are lovely."

Marlene giggled and pushed her chest forward. "Go
ahead. Someone in your condition shouldn't be denied a
little pleasure. Certainly you're not a virgin, are you?"

"Not exactly."

"What does that—" She felt his lips cover her breast,
then he began to suck on her like a child. "Oh, never
mind. Is it making you feel better?"

"Umm-humm!"

"Well have your fun."

Marlene began to wash his chest, then his stomach of
blood, dirt, and dust. He was really quite an Adonis with
the physique of a young Greek god. And when she dipped
her hand below the surface of the water, she found that
he had a huge erection.

"Well, my heavens! You aren't in nearly as bad a shape
as I'd thought." Her fingers gripped his long, stiff rod,
and she began to slide his foreskin up and down. "Feel
even better?"

"Ummm-hummm!"

Marlene laughed and pressed his face tightly against
her bosom because she was also feeling a whole lot better.
"The next thing I know, you're going to want me to scoot
up and sit in your lap."

"Oh, would you!" he cried, pulling his face away for a moment.

She studied him for a moment, then lifted herself up and gently eased down on his big tool. It slid in so nice and easy that she sighed and then settled down on him like a hen might a nest of eggs. "Well, sweet boy marshal, how is *that*?"

Dudley tore his mouth from her breast and kissed her on the lips, then winced with pain. His eyes were glassy but she could not tell if it was from the pleasure he was receiving or the blows to the head he'd taken or the liquor he'd consumed downstairs. But it didn't matter. He liked what he was doing and Marlene liked him doing it.

"Take your time, honey," she whispered. "The water will stay warm for quite a while. Just go nice and easy. That's it. That's it. In and out. Slow and easy. Oh, that feels *so* good!"

She threw her head back and pressed his poor face to her other breast. Rocking around and around and up and down, Marlene could feel a fire rising low in her belly. "I don't know what you meant when I asked you if you were a virgin and you said, 'not exactly,' but baby, you're doing everything just fine. Lovely, in fact. Don't hurry. Go slow and deep. Slow and . . . oh, yeah!"

They rocked and slipped and then locked and splashed water out of the tub as their passion increased. "Slower," she begged, clutching him tightly as he started to thrust harder. "Easy, lover, easy!"

Dudley was going out of his mind. He had never felt so alive and when he finally began to lose control, he raised her halfway out of the big cast iron tub and she rode him as he bucked and hollered and drove his rod ever deeper until he exploded and emptied himself completely. Marlene raked his back and told him what a wonderful lover he was and then she bit his shoulder and stiffened, crying out with pleasure and spilling waves of water onto her floor.

"My heavens, Dudley," she panted as they lay half submerged. "If I'd have been on the bottom, you'd probably have drowned me!"

"Oh, no I wouldn't have," he vowed. "Because I'd have wanted you so bad in the morning I'd have been more careful."

Marlene felt weak-kneed as she climbed off his big root, still so long and stiff that it poked up through the surface like a half submerged log. She found towels and dried them both off, then put Dudley to bed.

"Sweet young lover," she said as he closed his eyes and fell asleep almost instantly. "You're too nice and innocent to be a federal marshal."

She stood over the bed, watching him sleep. Then, she picked up his clothing intending to fold and put it away. The shirt, coat, and pants were completely ruined. No matter, she could go down to the merchantile in the morning and buy him new ones. She hoped he had some money and when she checked the inside of his pants pockets, she found a wad of bills.

"Good, I won't have to buy them out my money." Marlene unfolded the greenbacks and began to count. And count. And count. "Oh my god," she whispered. "You got just over a thousand dollars!"

She had never seen nearly so much money. She pressed it close to her ample bosom and closed her eyes. With this much money she could . . . go to California. Buy a home and maybe even a business. Turn respectable. Meet Lotta Crabtree or Lola Montez and get singing lessons. Become some famous . . . or at least respectable and happy.

With this much money, all her dreams could come true.

"I'm sorry. I hope you come from a rich family and I'm sure that is the case."

103

Marlene grabbed a satchel and emptied her shabby little dresser drawers. She fixed her hair and then stared at herself in the mirror.

"You're no good, Marlene. He'll hate you for this and you're taking more than money from him . . . you're taking his innocence and trust."

She wavered for a moment with indecision, then she whirled, bent over and kissed his sweet face. Tears filled her eyes but she straightened, squared her shoulders and went out the door. She knew how to leave a town in a hurry. This would not be the first, but it would be the last.

"Good-bye, lover," she called as she closed the door, looked up and down the hallway, and then headed for the back exit.

By morning, she would be high up in the Sierra Nevada Mountains and bound for the good life in sunny California.

Chapter 10

When Dudley awoke late the next morning, he felt as if his poor head would explode. And then, when he reached for his clothes and discovered that not only was Marlene missing, but so was his thousand dollars, he wished his head *had* exploded.

He dressed quickly and as he passed the cracked mirror in the little upstairs room, he saw his reflection. "Oh my gawd!" he cried. "I hardly recognize my own self!"

He rushed out into the hallway and then down the stairs to the bar where a new bartender and a few rough-looking customers were standing and talking.

"Marlene!" he panted. "Where did she go?"

"Isn't she upstairs?" the bartender, a fat man wearing a flannel shirt and black suspenders asked.

"No! I was upstairs in her room."

"Then I have no idea where she could have gone."

The bartender returned to his earlier conversation and appeared quite annoyed when Dudley hissed, "Look. She stole a lot of money from me last night. Where can I find her?"

"Who knows. Marlene don't work here. She comes and goes as she pleases. She rents that upstairs room once in a while. The boss don't ask her what she does when she takes men up there, but that ain't too hard to figure out."

A couple of the men chuckled and one, a tall, thin man with a drooping mustache and a bobbing Adam's apple said, "She never would take *me* up there. Would she take you, Luke?"

"Nope. And I begged her just like most of the fellas, but she wouldn't ever do it."

"But I have to get that money back!"

"Mister, I can't help you."

"Who can?"

"The boss lives over on Second Street. Little redbrick house with a railroad man's lantern hanging on the front porch. You can't miss it."

Dudley dashed outside, his head splitting with pain. He raced down to Second Street, and when he found the house, he beat furiously on its door until a nondescript woman in a housedress answered.

"What do you want?"

"I need to speak to the owner of the Waterhole."

"What about?"

"I was robbed by one of his girls. A woman named Marlene. She took me upstairs and—"

"I don't want to hear about it," the woman snapped. "Whatever happened to you up there is none of my business, and it also damn sure better not be any of my husband's business. So get along. William is asleep and doesn't like to be awakened until mid-afternoon."

"Please. Can you just tell me where I can find Marlene?"

"I don't even know who she is!" The woman glared. "But I say that, whatever she did to you, you had coming. Now get lost!"

An instant later, Dudley was staring at a closed door. Even more than that, he was wondering what Longarm would do or—

"Oh no! He's probably gone!"

Dudley turned and raced back up the street and he was badly winded and feeling as if he were going to faint by the time he reached the Dollar Livery. He skidded to a halt, caught his breath, then went looking for Salty Bates.

"I'm over here, dude!" the old livery man yelled. "You don't have to wake up the dead by all that hollerin'."

"Salty. Did someone take that ugly bay horse yet?"

"Sure. The big fella that rented the medicine wagon came along early this morning. I saw him driving the wagon out of town, must have been three hours ago."

Dudley groaned and leaned back against the wall of the barn. "I've really messed things up."

"What'd you do?"

"I met a girl."

"That's always the start of trouble."

"She was *different*."

"Sure she was. Was she the one that beat your face purple?"

"No. She took care of me last night. But when I woke up this morning, she had taken all my money. Salty, she stole a thousand dollars from me!"

The livery man whistled softly through his front teeth. "Whew! Boy, when you make a mistake, you really make it huge. I sure hope you got enough money to pay your board bill and all."

"I . . . I don't have any money at all."

Salty spit tobacco juice. "That does pose a problem. I ain't gonna let you get away with two more of my horses, a saddle, bridle blanket, and halter without payin' for 'em."

"Look. I can get the money from my family."

"Then do it."

"But I really would rather not ask for any more. Would you take something valuable in exchange?"

"Such as?"

107

"Such as—" Dudley thought hard. "How about my pocket watch? It's worth a hundred dollars easy and I'm amazed that, that . . . that woman didn't steal it as well."

"Let me see. It better be mighty fancy."

"It is," Dudley assured him. "It's a very expensive timepiece. Gold plated. Excellent workmanship. Fine gold-plated chain."

He dangled the watch in front of Salty and watched his eyes light up with desire. The deal was made and Dudley even walked away with thirty dollars cash.

"I'd better get busy and saddle up."

"The thing you'd better do is to buy some working clothes. Them that you're wearing are torn near to shreds. What did you get into a fight with last night, a grizzly bear?"

"No. There was this big brawl and well . . . I'd been drinking too much and things just went from bad to worse."

"The worse being when the woman stole all your daddy's money."

"That's right," Dudley said feeling shamed. "But I'll find her as soon as I take care of some other business. I'll find her for certain."

"If she's smart, she's left town with all that money," the old man decided out loud. "If she'd just stole ten or twenty dollars, I'd say she'd still be around. But a thousand . . . well, I'd say you are stuck."

"Don't tell me that," he groaned. A wave of dizziness overcame Dudley and he had to sit down.

"I got strong coffee in my room back in the barn," Salty offered. "Looks as if you could use some."

"Thanks. But I think I'd better go have a breakfast and buy some new clothes."

"Good idea. Buy some duds that don't make you look like an eastern dude. If you're a horse trader, you got to try and look like one. And given the condition of your face and your age, that won't be easy."

Dudley nodded and stumbled away, cradling his aching head. A few minutes later, just as he was about to enter the merchantile, a horseman came galloping up Virginia Street. His mount was heavily lathered and he seemed badly shaken. He drew his exhausted horse to a halt in front of the marshal's office and as he dismounted, he yelled, "Two more men have just been found murdered on the road up to Virginia City!"

Dudley halted in midstride. He gulped hard and then pivoted on his heel and headed back to the livery to claim his horses and tack. He would ride fast toward the Comstock Lode and hope to heaven that Longarm hadn't been involved in a shootout. Why, if he had, he might even have apprehended or killed the murderers!

What good would that do me? Dudley thought as he began to run again. Nothing. It would mean that this entire trip out west had been a monumental waste of time and a huge loss of money.

Chapter 11

When Dudley Applewhite hadn't showed up at the livery that morning as agreed, Longarm didn't waste any time looking for the young man. He figured that a United States Marshal, even an eighteen-year-old one, should have enough sense to take care of himself. If Dudley had hooked up with the wrong people, then he'd learn a tough lesson. If he'd just overslept, then perhaps it was for the best that they each went their own ways during the next few weeks.

Longarm had paid Otis Gilroy for his wagon and carefully counted out his fifty bottles of snake oil. He'd sampled a bottle and found it to be surprisingly good tasting.

"You'll sell every bottle and have 'em begging for more," Gilroy had promised. "Some of 'em will even get to feeling better and swear by this stuff."

"Just as long as I don't poison anyone," Longarm had told the man as he'd prepared to hitch up the ugly bay gelding and be on his way to the Comstock Lode.

"Don't be fooled by the looks of this horse," Salty had advised him. "If you need to ride him fast, he can run like a damned antelope."

"Sure," Longarm had called as he'd driven the rickety

old medicine wagon out of the livery yard and headed down Virginia Street.

He had only gone a few miles when he met a man galloping hard for town. The fellow had shouted, "Two more murders up on the Comstock Lode!"

Right then Longarm had been tempted to throw a saddle on the ugly bay gelding and put Salty's words to the test. But he'd checked that impulse, realizing that he'd spent a considerable amount of time and money to appear to be a medicine seller and it would be foolish to blow that cover just to arrive at the murder scene a bit quicker. Even so, he'd pushed the bay into a trot that had almost shaken the wagon to pieces and was soon climbing the long, winding road up to Virginia City. The traffic was heavy with supply wagons as well as miners and a colorful collection of travelers both on foot and on horseback.

The gelding threw itself into the work and Longarm quickly realized that the horse was no quitter. The wagon wasn't light and it probably should have been pulled by a two-horse team, but the bay was surprisingly strong and they made steady progress until they arrived at a spot where Longarm pulled over and let the bay catch its breath. He filled a bucket of water from an oak barrel tied to the wagon and watered the sweaty gelding.

"It won't be much longer of a pull," he promised, gazing back down upon the valley and farther out to the snowcapped Sierras. "Another mile or two, if I remember correctly."

The bay drank every drop from the bucket, and when it was dry, Longarm climbed back up onto the driver's seat and continued the steep, winding ascent until he finally topped the grade and the road became flat as it wound its way through the rough, dry country dotted with cedar and pinion pine. Now he began to see hundreds of tailings that marked where the Comstock miners were digging. Some of the claims had been abandoned but most of them were still being worked and Longarm could see sheltering tents and brush arbors along with wash lines and all manner of junk. Rusting tin cans and the glass shards of broken bottles glittered off all the hillsides, and far up ahead he could see smoke trailing up from the tower of a shelter. He had heard that the Comstock Lode was declining, but it seemed as busy and frantic as ever.

He rounded a curve in the road and saw a large knot of men collected up by a huge tailing that marked a deep and well-worked mine shaft. The men all seemed to be standing around an object and Longarm figured that this would be the scene of the recent murder.

"Whoa up," he said, pulling the wagon off to the side of the road so that he would not block traffic.

The bay seemed only too happy to stop and wait as Longarm set his brake, dismounted, and slowly trudged up the sage-covered hillside to join the gathering of somber men.

"What's going on?" he asked.

A fellow with a derby hat turned to him and, wiping tears from his eyes replied in a bitter voice, "Someone killed Ollie and Jess early this morning. Cut their throats while they slept and made off with their gold. Ollie and Jess were both good men. Now we're all afraid the same thing will happen to us unless we figure out who to catch and hang."

"Any clues?"

The man bit his lower lip and was obviously struggling not to lose his composure. "Not that I know of. We all work in this same area but we keep to ourselves pretty much until evening. It's hard, solitary work. Jess and Ollie were doing real good, though. We knew they had struck a little vein because they'd been buying most of the drinks at night. And when a fella's money ran out and he got

113

low on grub, them boys were always willing to give him some help."

Another man, overhearing this conversation said, "They were good fellas. The best. Whoever done this had to have sneaked right up through the middle of our claims in the middle of the night." He glanced up at the sun. "It's nearly noon. They both look like they've been dead for quite a few hours."

Longarm's eyes traveled past the onlookers to the two corpses laid out on blankets. Both of their faces were unnaturally pale, as would be expected, and both had horrible slashes across their throats. The blood in their beards and on their shirts was caked and dark. Flies were swarming and Longarm knew that they would have to be buried before sundown, given the heat of the day.

Had he been in his normal capacity as a federal marshal, he would have stepped forward and began to question the mourners in some detail, but that wasn't possible, so he moved around on the fringes of the gathering asking questions, seeking any kind of clues as to the identity of the killer or killers.

"Did anyone see any footprints or horse tracks?" he asked a tall, shabbily dressed man who stood with clenched fists and a grief-stricken expression.

The man shook his head. "We didn't think to look until so many were gathered here. Bennie was the first to come over and investigate when we didn't see any sign of Ollie or Jess long after they normally would have been dumpin' rock and dirt over the side of this claim. He commenced to hollerin' like he'd gone crazy and we all knew something was bad wrong. So we dropped our picks and shovels and come running. Of course, we couldn't do no good. And by the time we all realized what had happened, we'd stomped all over this camp."

"That's a shame," Longarm said. "Did anybody see any

strangers around here last evening or even in the last couple of days?"

"I didn't and I work just over there." The man pointed a shaky finger toward his nearby claim. "If there'd been strangers about, they would have stuck out like a sore thumb. People don't mess around among the claims or they could get lead poisoning. We all watch out for each other from sunrise to sundown."

"Well," Longarm said, "someone must have known about Ollie and Jess having hit pay dirt and that they could rob them of a lot of ore."

"I expect so," the man said. "Who are *you*?"

"I'm selling a healing elixir," Longarm told him. "It's guaranteed to kill worms, fleas, and dissolve any impurities in your blood."

"You don't say."

"That's right. It's good for rheumatism and painful joints, headaches, and back strains and bad feet."

"For a fact?"

Longarm jerked a thumb over his shoulder toward his wagon pulled off the road below. "That's right."

The man's eyes narrowed. "Why that's old Otis Gilroy's medicine wagon."

"It is," Longarm admitted. "Otis got real drunk and sick then let me take over his business for a while."

"I liked Otis's medicine. Tastes real good. Is yours the same?"

"It is," Longarm replied. "Same tried and proven cure for about anything that ails a man."

"Well, I could use a bottle pretty quick," the fellow said, licking his lips. "This whole murder thing has really got me feeling low. I expect some of these other boys feel the same way. Ollie and Jess were well liked by everyone on the Comstock Lode."

"Not quite," Longarm told the man as he stared at the two dead men.

"Yeah. I see what you mean."

Longarm moved through the crowd, hearing the talk and hoping to learn something of value. Some of the prospectors were just plain angry and talking about finding the killer even though they hadn't any idea of how or where to begin. Others were simply grieving and a couple off to one side were quietly speculating on who would get the deceased's rich claim.

When he was certain that no one had any idea who might have committed the heinous crimes, he detached himself from them and began to walk a perimeter around the claim. From what he could see, there was mining activity below and on both sides, but the area above Ollie and Jess's claim was open and leading up to the crown of a sage and rock-covered hilltop.

Longarm hiked up to the top of the hill, thinking that whoever had committed the crime must have also realized the safest way to reach the two dead miners was to come over the top of the hill and sneak down into their camp.

"Yep," he said, finding a place among the brown rocks where someone had obviously whiled away a good amount of time. Longarm reached that deduction by noting how someone had obviously laid a blanket on the dirt and then smoked cigarette after cigarette.

Hand-rolled with brown paper.

Longarm twisted around and gazed back down at the crowd. Yep, he thought, it wouldn't be hard to sneak down there and slit a couple of throats without being seen or heard. But how would the killer get away with money and a large amount of gold ore? It would be heavy, wouldn't it?

In the years that Longarm had worked solving crimes and tracking down thieves, murders and all other manner of outlaws, he'd come to the conclusion that those type of people were usually indolent and no account. Most of those that committed robberies were just too damn lazy to succeed by their own efforts. That being the case, Longarm doubted that whoever had killed Ollie and Jess had been willing to haul a heavy sack of gold very far.

I think I'd better go over the top and have a look down the other side of this hill, he decided.

Sure enough, he did not have to go more than fifty feet before he discovered where the murderer had tied a horse. A horse with a corrective shoe that left no doubt that this was his man.

Longarm squatted down in the dirt and studied the unusual hoofprint for several long minutes just so he'd imprint it indelibly in his mind. He also used his hand to measure the length of the boot tracks he found and they exactly matched his own.

"He's a big fella all right." Longarm collected one of the brown cigarette butts. He sniffed the remaining shreds of dark tobacco and slipped it into his vest pocket.

He searched the area and then followed the tracks a few hundred yards until he was certain that they were headed toward Virginia City. That was where he hoped to find his killer.

The miners had begun to dig their friends a pair of graves. Longarm tipped his hat in a gesture of respect to the two dead men. From what he could see and what he'd heard, Ollie and Jess had been fine men and certainly had not deserved to die choking in their own blood.

"I'm going to get the one that killed you boys," Longarm said under his breath as he headed down to the road and his medicine wagon. "I'm going to get him today if I get lucky."

Chapter 12

Virginia City was losing some of its former luster. The big saloons like the Bucket of Blood and the Silver Dollar were still crowded with miners, but Longarm could see that some of the smaller saloons and establishments had closed. That was the way of mining towns . . . they sprang up suddenly and their time was generally short. Some didn't even last a full year, but Virginia City had been going for decades.

He drove up C Street past the old Territorial Enterprise office, where the famed Mark Twain had once been employed and where the venerable Dan DeQuille could still be found grinding out his daily quota of copy. As he drove along, several people called out for him to stop and sell them bottles of his elixir and Longarm would have obliged except that the traffic was heavy and he didn't want to cause a bottleneck. Longarm noted the marshal's office and wondered what kind of officials worked there these days. In the past when he'd had occasion to visit this famous mining town, he'd discovered that the law in Virginia City was either on the take from greedy mine owners and operators, or totally inept. And those men who

119

had apparently tried to be honest had been gunned down or soon run out of town.

Virginia City is looking tired and a little frayed around the edges, he thought. But there's a killer here someplace and I mean to find him if it is humanly possible.

Longarm turned up a side street and tied his wagon up next to a vacant brick building, thinking that there was only one way to have any chance of catching his killer, and that was by finding his horse. Reno's Marshal Ralph Benson had said that the horse in question might be a buckskin. If so, such a colored horse with a corrective bar shoe would be a whole lot easier to identify.

Before leaving, Longarm watered the weary bay gelding, promising he'd be back in a few hours to hunt the animal up a livery where he'd be fed and rubbed down for his admirable effort in pulling the wagon up the long, steep grade.

Then Longarm took off in search of a buckskin with a odd-shaped shoe. He started at the liveries, using the ruse that he was looking to buy a horse and preferred buckskins. Two hours later, he hadn't found his horse and there were no more liveries in town. Well, he'd hoped this would be easy but, as usual, it would not.

Tired and a little footsore from all his walking up and down the steep streets in Virginia City, he stepped inside the Lucky Lady Saloon and ordered a beer.

"Did you hear about the two miners getting their throats cut last night?" he asked the bartender who served him.

"I sure didn't. You say two more got murdered?"

Conversation all along the bar died and Longarm knew he had everyone's full attention. "That's right. I drove up from Reno today and came upon a crowd of men about two miles north of here. They were all gathered around a pair of dead miners."

"You catch their names?"

"Ollie and Jess," Longarm said.

120

"Damn!" the bartender swore. "Those were some of my best customers. A pair of nicer fellas you'd be hard-pressed to find. And you say that their throats were cut?"

"I'm afraid so."

The bartender turned to his other customers. "Everyone hear that?"

The men nodded in silence.

"I'm pouring one on the house in memory of Ollie and Jess!"

Glasses were emptied then hit the bar top as the bottle made its way down the line making refills. Longarm took his along with the rest, and when the toast was made, he drank his glass dry.

"Mister," the bartender said, "I seem to recall your face but your name escapes me."

"Custis," he said, not giving his last name or his business. "And I'm sure sorry about those two. I guess you folks up here have got some kind of murderer on the loose, huh?"

"We sure do," the bartender said, pouring himself another drink and leaning forward on his elbows. "And damned if anyone can catch the sonofabitch that's doing the killing. We don't even know if it's one man or several. The killings just happen all over the territory. I can tell you that the people up here are pretty spooked. I wouldn't be surprised if innocent people start getting accused and maybe even shot."

"What about the local authorities?"

The bartender scoffed. "Hell, Marshal Quinn Rucker and Deputy Orvis Boone don't even own horses! They just parade around town throwin' drunks in jail and collecting fines. They're in it strictly for the money. You won't find them poking around the hills trying to solve these murders."

"I've heard rumors that the murderer rides a buckskin horse," Longarm said loud enough to be overheard by most of the patrons. "Anybody else hear that rumor?"

The men leaning along the bar nursing their free drinks shook their heads.

"Well," Longarm mused aloud. "Buckskins aren't rare, but neither are they common."

"I know three or four fellas that own buckskins," a man said. "But they're all good men. I sure hope you don't start no rumors and get them into trouble. As nervous as folks are around here, they're likely to jump to all kinds of wrong conclusions."

"You make a good point," Longarm agreed. "But that is what I heard. Big man on a buckskin horse."

"That could be fifty men in these parts," the bartender said. "I sure am sorry to hear about Ollie and Jess. I'd guess that whoever cut their throats got away with a lot of gold. I once asked Jess if he and his partner were putting their gold into the bank where it'd be safe. Know what they said?"

"No."

"They said they had such good friends that they didn't need to worry about a thing. Said that no one would steal from them 'cause they had so many friends and no enemies. I told Jess that a bag or two of gold was mighty tempting and that he ought to put it in the bank. But Jess just laughed. He didn't take much serious. He and Ollie were generous to a fault, and you'd never meet two harder-working men. They're gonna be missed, gawd dammit!"

Two of the patrons nodded, and the taller of the pair said, "I think we ought to all go over to the marshal's office and demand that he and his worthless damned deputy go out there and start hunting down whoever is doing these killings. And by gawd, if they refuse . . . I say we ought to run them two worthless bastards right of out town!"

Suddenly, everyone seemed to think that was a great

idea. Longarm just stood aside and watched as the crowd fed on its own anger. And when the saloon emptied and everyone headed off to confront Marshal Rucker and Deputy Boone, Longarm fell in behind, wondering what would happen. He hoped that the marshal would be smart enough to agree to at least go out and investigate the deaths, even if it was just an act. Because, if he wasn't that smart, he and his deputy could be in deep trouble. This mining town was on edge and something had to be done or innocent men could get hurt and maybe even hanged. Vigilante justice was always born out of frustration, and when it turned ugly, it could become blind to truth.

The crowd swelled as it marched down C Street. The word seemed to sweep ahead of them and men began to pour out of saloons and businesses either out of curiosity or real anger. As they neared the marshal's office, Longarm was beginning to get worried. If Rucker wasn't a savvy veteran, things could get completely out of hand.

If they do, he thought, I'll have to step in and help the marshal and his deputy even though it would mean giving up my cover. I just couldn't stand by and let them get mobbed.

He passed the side street where he'd left the medicine wagon and glanced up to see how his ugly bay was doing.

The horse was eating a bush, but the wagon was . . . was *gone*!

Longarm raced up the hill to look around in every direction. The bay kept on eating the bush as if nothing in the world was wrong.

"Damn it!" Longarm swore. "Someone stole everything!"

He kicked a rock down the street and swore a blue streak, none of which helped in the least. He should have known that, with fifty bottles of almost straight alcohol, someone would break into the wagon and steal his contents. But the entire wagon in broad daylight? How brazen had criminals become in this town?

"Come on," he snapped, grabbing the bay's reins and leading it back down to C Street. "You're not worth much but you're all I have left."

The bay snorted and plodded along behind as Longarm hurried to catch up with the crowd. He would search for the medicine wagon later, but right now, he needed to be close to the marshal's office just in case things turned real ugly and the angry mob got totally out of hand.

Longarm tied the bay to a hitch rail and hurried over to stand at the back of the crowd. Being taller than almost everyone, he had a clear view of the two lawmen standing before their office and he could hear their voices trying to be heard.

"Let 'em have their say!" a man shouted, raising his six-gun and firing it into the sky. "Let the marshal talk!"

The crowd fell into a restless, sullen silence. Marshal Rucker was a tall, slender, and nondescript man wearing a rumpled black suit coat, white shirt, and tie. His only unusual feature was a pair of ears that stuck straight out under the brim of his hat and the pearl-handled pistol strapped to his narrow waist. Deputy Orvis Boone, on the other hand, had the look of a man to be reckoned with in a fight. He was big and broad-shouldered. Thick legs planted apart, he stood glaring out at the mob giving the impression that he was more annoyed than afraid.

"Listen up, you men!" Marshal Rucker shouted, raising his hands. "I know that you are all frustrated and angry over these killings. But my job—and Deputy Boone's job—is to protect the citizens of *Virginia City*. We can't be everywhere at once."

Rucker waved his arms in a big circle and continued, his voice entreating everyone to be reasonable. "Why, there are thousands of mining claims and tens of thousands of acres of land all around, and how do you men expect us to protect it all and, at the same time, uphold law and order in Virginia City!"

"Well, something is by-gawd got to be done to stop these killings!" a burly and red-faced miner shouted. "And I think it's high time that we the people took this matter into our own damn hands!"

"No!" Rucker cried. "What you are talking about here is vigilante justice."

"That's right! It worked over in the California gold fields. We strung up a'plenty of murderers and thieves and every last one of them deserved it!"

The crowd roared in approval and several of the more intoxicated participants began to shout for a hanging rope, as if they had some rational idea of who to hang.

"Now listen here," Deputy Boone shouted. "Me and the marshal aren't paid enough to go racin' around in the sagebrush looking for whoever is doing the murders!"

Longarm groaned because that was the very last thing that should have been said. And as he expected, it fueled the anger of the crowd, which suddenly surged forward. Too late, the marshal and his deputy tried to retreat back into the safety of their office. The crowd was on them and Longarm saw fists rise and fall and he knew that the lawmen were being beaten senseless.

"Damn it!" Longarm hissed, knowing he had no choice but to try to save the marshal and his foolish deputy and, therefore, toss aside his facade of being a snake oil peddler. But then, he'd just been robbed of his wagon and medicine, so what was there to lose?

Longarm bulled forward, grabbing and tossing men aside in his wake. When he reached the two fallen lawmen, they were on their backs and already beaten bloody. The incensed miners had swarmed all over them and were taking out their frustration, one smashing blow at a time.

Longarm drew his pistol and cracked one powerful fellow across the back of his head. The man slumped forward and Longarm pistol-whipped a second man. When a third turned and tried to grab his gun, Longarm broke his nose with a vicious backhand swing.

Suddenly, everyone jumped back and Longarm surged to his feet, tearing his badge from his pocket and holding it up so that it glinted brightly in the sun.

"I'm a United States Deputy Marshal and I will kill any man who tries to interfere with me. Is that understood!"

The crowd recoiled and Longarm knew that he still didn't have the situation anywhere close to being under control. "I have come all the way from Denver to help you people find out who is murdering and robbing in this part of Nevada. If you want justice, then stand back and let me go to work for you!"

"You said you were a damned snake oil peddler," said someone he recognized from the Lucky Lady Saloon. "Which is it, Mister! Lawman or peddler?"

"I'm a lawman."

"Well what are you going to do to stop the killings!" a man shouted. "Or are you just another *town* lawman?"

"I'll go wherever and do whatever it takes to find out who is responsible for these murders and robberies. I won't leave until the killer is either dead or standing before a court of law who will most certainly sentence him to hang by the neck."

Longarm's eyes raked the crowd and they backed away. "All right then," he said. "We need a doctor!"

"I'll go see if Doc Bartlett is sober."

"Do that," Longarm said. "And bring him even if he's drunk! We got men here that need medical attention!"

The crowd slowly dispersed and when Longarm was sure that the danger was past, he knelt beside the two lawmen. Marshal Quinn Rucker was unconscious and blood was trickling out of both his protruding ears. His

126

nose had been smashed into his face, his front teeth were broken, and his condition was desperate.

Big Deputy Orvis Boone was in much better shape. He'd rolled onto his stomach and covered his head with his hands. He was bloodied but able to sit up and spit blood. "I'm gonna get even with them that did this to us," he vowed. "I know who it was that did it and I'll get them one by one."

"No, you won't," Longarm told the deputy. "What you are going to do is to go inside your office, clean up, and assume the duties of town marshal because Rucker is finished."

"He wasn't worth much anyway," Boone hissed, spitting more blood. "I did all the dirty work and he got most of the money."

Longarm didn't know what that meant and he figured this was no time to ask questions. Instead, he examined the heads of the two men that he'd pistol-whipped.

"I hope you killed 'em," Boone spat. "Them bastards were trying to kill me."

"I didn't kill them, but they're going to be out of commission for a while just like your friend Marshal Rucker . . . if he even survives."

"He ain't my friend," the deputy said, swaying to his feet. "He's a damn fool. If I'd been marshal this wouldn't have happened. I'd have did as they asked and saved ourselves a beating. Rucker was stupid and he almost got us both killed."

"You're right," Longarm agreed, surprised by the venom that the deputy was directing toward his marshal. "Let's get Rucker inside and clean him up before the doctor arrives."

"You clean him up if you want," Boone snapped. "I'm going to take care of myself. And I sure don't appreciate no federal officer coming in here where he don't belong."

Longarm started to argue and then thought, to hell with

it. He'd straighten out Deputy Boone later . . . even get him removed from office if that was possible.

He grabbed the unconscious marshal under his arms and dragged him into the office. The only bunk inside was in the only jail cell, so Longarm hauled Rucker over to it and laid him down. He spotted a pitcher of water and some wash towels and set about cleaning the poor man's battered face. Marshal Rucker was moaning and it was clear that he had suffered a concussion and probably some broken ribs.

Longarm had seen a lot of beaten men but none any worse than Rucker. He figured it was a coin toss as to whether the man would live . . . or die.

Chapter 13

Dr. Bartlett arrived only minutes later. He was a rumpled, heavy man with a wild shock of silver hair, and thick, round spectacles. He carried a worn leather medical bag in one of his pudgy hands and a stethoscope dangled from the other. The man wasted no words on Longarm but hurried into the cell and stood for a moment, gazing down at Marshal Rucker.

"Dear god," he whispered, "I don't think I've ever seen a human so badly beaten."

Longarm stood beside the cell door. "His breathing sounds terrible. I expect he has a few broken ribs."

The doctor unbuttoned Rucker's vest, then his shirt. When he began to touch the marshal's ribs, Rucker recoiled. The doctor placed his stethoscope on the marshal's laboring chest and listened for several moments.

"Well?" Longarm asked.

"I don't think any of the broken ribs punctured his lungs. No sign of bright red blood on his lips, is there?"

"Not that I've seen."

Bartlett placed his hands on Rucker's face, one on each side of the smashed nose. He shook his head and then pressed inward. Longarm heard the marshal's nose crack as a fresh torrent of blood poured out. But the nose was straight now and the doctor asked for a pan of cool water.

"Where's Deputy Boone?" he asked.

"I don't know," Longarm answered.

"Is he also hurt?"

"Yes, but not nearly as bad. He rolled over on his stomach and covered his face when the crowd landed on them. He knew how to protect himself."

"Figures," the doctor said. "That one has been in bad scrapes before. But the marshal didn't know any better."

Longarm brought a pan of water and the doctor began to wash away the fresh blood. "Might be some permanent ocular damage."

"What?"

"This man's right eye has been gouged," Bartlett said, using his thumb to lift Rucker's eyelid. "You can see the eye is a mess."

Longarm nodded and looked away. Marshal Rucker's right eye had the look of a squashed cherry.

"Could be some bleeding in the skull," Bartlett muttered more to himself than to Longarm. "Severe concussion at the least."

"What are his chances?"

"I think he'll survive," the doctor said. "But wouldn't bet on it."

"Do you want us to move him over to your office?"

Bartlett shook his head. "My office isn't this nice. Besides, I'm afraid that any further movement might cause one of those broken ribs to shift and puncture the lung. If that happened . . ."

Dr. Bartlett didn't need to elaborate. Longarm could see that the situation was critical.

"Can you stay with him?" Longarm asked.

"Of course. The next twenty-four hours are critical. If he survives them, then I'd say his chances are much improved." The doctor looked up from his patient. "What on earth triggered the crowd?"

"It was Deputy Boone," Longarm replied. "He had to butt in and give his two cents worth and that really made everyone mad. They just snapped and swarmed all over both men. I couldn't reach them in time to keep it from happening."

"And who are you?"

"Deputy Marshal Custis Long. I'm here to get to the bottom of all these murders."

"Good luck."

Bartlett's tired old face was cross-stitched with a maze of tiny blue blood vessels and his nose had the familiar reddish hue of a hard, two-fisted drinker. You didn't have to be a mind reader to see that Dr. Bartlett's life had failed badly to measure up to his early expectations.

Longarm waited until the doctor had finished doing everything possible for Marshal Rucker and then had exited the cell. Then, he motioned the physician to a seat at Deputy Boone's desk. "Do you know anything about all the murders and robberies?"

"I know that the killer likes to cut his victim's throats. He's also fond of torturing them." Bartlett rubbed a shaky hand across his eyes and removed a pint bottle of whiskey from his medical kit. Without looking at Longarm, he uncorked the bottle and took a long, shuddering swig. Then, he carefully replaced the cork and sighed with relief.

"Doc, that stuff is going to be the death of you."

"Nobody lives forever, young man." He raised a finger and pointed it at Longarm, squinting with one eye as if he were aiming a pistol. "Least of all a lawman."

"I'm not too worried," Longarm said. "From what little I know about the killer, he only robs people with lots of gold, valuables, or cash."

"Yes," the doctor said, lowering his finger. "So that

leaves both of us out of the equation. But whoever is doing these murders is clearly crazy. He's a demon and demons are unpredictable. Were I you, Marshal Long, I would not feel entirely safe."

"What do you know about the murders?" Longarm asked with a hint of impatience.

"I know that the killer is a very powerful man. I have examined the bodies of his victims and I have seen that he is capable of cutting through gristle and bone. And that requires an extremely sharp knife as well as a muscular arm. I'd say the victim would be a large man, one approximately your own size."

"Fine," Longarm said. "But have you seen anything on the corpses you have examined that might help me catch this maniac?"

"Did you know that he severs the fingers of his victims when he is otherwise unable to extract a valuable ring?"

"No, I didn't."

"It has happened twice to my knowledge. One ring was encrusted with real diamonds. Small ones encircling a ruby. In the second instance, the ring had five very large diamonds. I know this because their friends described the missing jewelry in some detail."

"Now *that* is very interesting," Longarm said, thinking that the killer might be stupid enough to actually wear such rings. "Anything else?"

"The killer is a tobacco fiend. He smokes hand-rolled cigarettes."

"I know. With brown paper."

"Not always," Bartlett countered. "I've seen white paper wrappers littering the scene of the crime."

"Oh," was all that Longarm could say. "Anything else?"

"Yes. The killer is pigeon-toed."

"What?"

"You heard me. He walks with his toes pointed inward.

It's pronounced enough that you'd notice if you were really looking."

Longarm thought back to where he'd found the killer's footprints up in the sage and cedar overlooking Ollie and Jess's mining claim. Yes, he thought, and I should have noted that on my own. This doctor looks like a drunk but his mind is still very sharp and observant.

"Doctor, you're being very helpful. Do you have anything else that might help me catch this killer?"

"I have my own theories," Doctor Bartlett said. "For instance . . . hello Boone. I didn't see you standing there. Come on inside."

The deputy pushed through the doorway. His face had a lopsided appearance due to extreme and uneven swelling. One of his eyes was nearly shut and his lips were purple and puffy. He wore a bandage taped to his forehead.

"Where have you been?" Longarm bluntly asked.

"I knew Doc would be busy fixin' up the marshal so I went and found someone to take care of me right away." Boone moved over to the cell and stared at the marshal. "Is he going to make it?"

"I don't know," the doctor replied. "Depends on how much swelling his brain might have to do."

"He doesn't look to me like he'll live," Boone said, turning away and coming back to lean against his desk. "I never liked Rucker, but he sure didn't deserve what he got outside. Neither did I, for that matter."

Longarm wanted to disagree. To his way of thinking, Boone was at least partly responsible for inciting the crowd to violence.

"I expect you to watch over Marshal Rucker when Dr. Bartlett isn't here," Longarm said.

"I don't care what you expect," Boone told him as he removed his badge and tossed it on his desk. "I'm quitting. Damned if I'll work under a federal lawman who

133

don't know his butt from his boot when it comes to the problems we face up here on the Comstock Lode."

It was all that Longarm could do not to jump up and inflict some more damage on Boone's brutish and battered face. "Get out of here."

"I got pay coming."

"You won't find it here," Longarm said, pushing out of his chair and standing up to the former deputy. "And I don't much care for a man who shoots his mouth off the way you did outside. I don't know if you are just stupid or what, but I doubt that crowd would have gone crazy if you'd kept quiet."

"Blaming me, huh?" Boone asked. "Well, that's about what I'd expect from a fed. Maybe when I heal a little you'd like to try to arrest me. Huh?"

"I will if you break the law."

Boone sneered with contempt. "I was the only law in Virginia City. You can ask anybody who kept the peace. It sure wasn't Rucker. Hell, he didn't want to leave the safety of this office! But I wasn't afraid to go out there at night and keep things under control. And did I get any thanks? Hell, no!"

Boone turned on his heel and marched over to a rifle rack. He grabbed the best weapon, a Winchester. "If the city council ever gets around to paying me my back wages, they can have this rifle. If not, I reckon it will about make us even."

Longarm started to step into Boone's path, but Dr. Bartlett caught his sleeve and hissed, "Let him go, Marshal. You've got enough trouble and there's no one to replace you if he busts you up."

"Yeah," Longarm replied, sitting down again and watching Boone head out the door. "I guess you're right."

"Of course I am."

Longarm closed his eyes for a moment. He had a pounding headache, his feet hurt from all the walking, and his stomach was growling with hunger. "Doc," he said, "this has been a long, tough day. I got my wagon stolen and I have a horse to take care of before I even start to think of myself. After that, I'm going to get some food and some sleep."

"Then go ahead," Bartlett urged. "I'm good for three or four hours. Bring me back something to eat and I'll stay here with Quinn until morning."

"Are you sure?"

"Yeah." Bartlett reached into his medical kit and extracted his bottle of whiskey. He held it up to the light of the window and his lips pursed in deep thought. "I think I'm going to need another before morning, though."

"Doc, I—"

"Here," the doctor interrupted, dragging out some wadded bills from his pockets. "This will more than cover for me."

Longarm took the man's money and headed left. After finding the bay a good livery where the ugly but big-hearted animal could receive its well-deserved rest, Longarm enjoyed a steak dinner and a glass of beer at a small restaurant that he'd enjoyed in the past. Feeling better, he asked the cook to pack up some food for Doc Bartlett. He made one more stop at a saloon and bought a pint of whiskey before heading back to the marshal's office.

"Doc?" he called as he entered.

The doctor was gone. Longarm placed his food and whiskey on Boone's desk and scratched his head wondering where the physician had disappeared. *He's probably gone to the crapper or stepped around the building to take a leak.*

Longarm sat down to wait for Bartlett's return. After all his exertions and the big meal, his eyes were heavy with the need for sleep. Moments later, he dozed off in Marshal Rucker's office chair, his feet propped up on the man's desk.

"Marshal?"

Longarm's eyes popped open and he jumped.

"Easy," Bartlett said. "You just dozed off."

Longarm knuckled his eyes. He realized that it was dark outside. "How long were you gone?"

The doctor sat down and opened the food that Longarm had brought for him. He seemed unsteady and Longarm smelled whiskey all over the man. "Did you go to a saloon?" he asked, trying not to accuse.

"Well, yes," the man admitted. "But that's not why I left the marshal unattended."

"Then *why* did you leave before I returned?"

"Someone burst in here and claimed a man had been stabbed in the Bucket of Blood. But, when I went there, there was no stabbing, so I had a drink or two and came right back. I wasn't gone more than half an hour."

Bartlett opened his medical kit and retrieved his whiskey. He took a long pull, then smacked his porcine lips. "Ahhh, that's better."

"How is Marshal Rucker doing?"

"Hmmm. Guess I better check up on him. It's been a while."

Longarm followed the unsteady doctor over to the cell and watched him go inside and lean over the still unconscious marshal.

"Well?" Longarm asked when Bartlett inhaled sharply. "How is he doing?"

"He's . . . he's dead."

"Damn!"

Bartlett seemed to shake all over and then he collapsed beside the cell cot and the body it supported.

"Doc? Are you all right?"

"No," Bartlett said in a voice that shook. "I'm not!"

"You did all that you could. Didn't you?"

"Yes, but—"

"Then you can't blame yourself for the man's death.

136

You said that he might have brain damage and internal bleeding."

"Yes, Marshal Long," the doctor said, his face drained of color, "but unless I'm mistaken—and that is possible— this man died of *forcible suffocation*!"

Chapter 14

Longarm just didn't know what to say or think about Marshal Rucker maybe being suffocated. But there was no question that he'd died awake. His mouth was wide open as were his eyes and even though they were glazed over in death, you could see that they were filled with stark terror.

"Doc," he said, "it's getting late, and this has been one hell of a bad day. Three men dead and someone stole my wagon."

"Well," Bartlett replied, "it works that way sometimes. And I could be wrong about the cause of the marshal's death."

Longarm shook his head. "If he *was* suffocated, who would do such a thing?"

"I have no idea."

"Deputy Boone?"

"I doubt it. There was no love between them, but Boone is not a murderer."

"Are you sure about that?"

"Yes. He's oafish and crude and not particularly bright, that's obvious. But a murderer? Well, slashing throats is not his style."

"Then who could have smothered Marshal Rucker?"

"Anyone watching from outside would have known the marshal was alone when I went rushing off to the Bucket of Blood."

"Who gave you that message?" Longarm asked. "That's where we can start to untangle this mess."

"I don't know."

"What does that mean?"

"It means," the doctor said, "that someone stuck his head in the door and shouted the message. He was gone before I could even turn my head."

Longarm gritted his teeth in frustration. "I think I'll call it a day and find a place to sleep. Maybe I'll have some questions for you in the morning."

"Don't ask them before ten o'clock," Bartlett told him, not needing to explain that he'd be incapacitated with his usual morning hangover.

Longarm headed out the door feeling as if the day had been a disaster. Tomorrow he would again scour the town in search of a buckskin—or any horse for that matter— with a bar crossed corrective horseshoe. He'd learned from long and hard experience that persistence was the key to success. If a man didn't get too discouraged and he kept trying, generally things worked out in his favor.

"Pssst!"

Longarm turned to see Dudley Applewhite standing in the shadows. He joined him saying, "What are you doing here? I thought you might still be sleeping it off down in Reno."

"Look. I'm sorry about missing your farewell but I had some trouble."

"Oh?"

"Someone stole a thousand dollars from me! It was all the money that my father had telegraphed from Boston."

Longarm whistled softly. "And how did *that* happen?"

"That's not important," Dudley said too quickly.

"Sure it is," Longarm insisted. "You're a federal marshal. Did you catch the thief?"

"No."

"Well how come? He's probably—"

"It was a woman," Dudley said. "A beautiful young lady, actually."

Longarm couldn't help but chuckle. "Ah, now I begin to get the picture. She got you drunk then rolled you. Dudley, why aren't I surprised at this piece of sad news?"

"Look, damn it! I learned a hard lesson. Okay? And as soon as we catch the killer we're after, I'm going to find Marlene and get my money back."

"Sure you will."

There was a moment of strained silence, then Dudley asked, "I saw you come out of the marshal's office. What happened?"

Longarm quickly related the day's misfortunes and ended by saying, "And to top it off, someone stole my medicine wagon."

It was Dudley's turn to laugh. "So you lost an *entire* wagon!"

"I'll find it."

"Sure you will."

"Shut up," Longarm snapped. "I'm going to get a hotel and get some sleep."

"So you had to reveal that you are really a marshal, huh?"

"That's right."

"Then," Dudley said, "I might as well drop this nonsense of being a horse trader."

"No," Longarm told him. "You could be my ace in the hole."

"What does that mean?"

"It means that, if someone really did go into Rucker's office and smother him while the doctor and I were out, then they are watching me. And, if that is the case, it also

141

means that they are going to be very difficult to trap and that I could be in some danger."

"So that's where I come in?"

"Yes," Longarm said. "You're our element of surprise. It means that you are going to have to cover my back."

"I see," Dudley said, nodding with understanding. "You're telling me that, if the killer really did smother Marshal Rucker, you could be next."

"Exactly. He wouldn't try to smother me, of course, but I'm sure I'm a target for ambush. And tomorrow, I'll be making the rounds again and searching for that horse with the bar under its shoe."

"Want me to do the same?"

"I'd rather you shadowed me and pay particular attention if anyone seems to be watching my moves."

"I can do that."

"Are you sure that you won't get involved with some gal and wind up getting rolled . . . or worse?"

"Of course not! I've learned an expensive lesson. And besides, who are you to get after me. I lost money, but you lost an entire medicine wagon!"

Longarm had to concede the point. "There's a hotel just up the street called the Ore House."

"Cute," Dudley told him.

"That's where I'll get a room."

"What about me?"

"Are you broke?"

"No," Dudley answered, "but I'm not exactly flush, either."

"Then I suggest you get a room at the Buckshot Hotel. It's cheap and I've been told that it is not too flea-ridden."

"Thanks a lot!"

"And stay away from the saloon girls," Longarm warned as he stepped back out on the boardwalk and headed down the street.

• • •

The Ore House was a stately Victorian mansion that had been converted into an upper-class hotel. It had been built by one of the overnight millionaires on the Comstock who had almost as quickly lost his money on high-flying mining stocks. It was a two-story structure surrounded by an ornamental iron fence that must have cost a fortune all by itself. The rooms were expensive, even by Comstock Lode standards, but Longarm felt safe there and he figured that, after a day such as he'd just endured, he deserved a good, safe room.

Stepping up on the front porch, he was just about to enter the Ore House when he caught a shadowy movement out of the corner of his eye. Drawing his gun, Longarm whirled and found himself face-to-face with a woman whose body he well remembered from the last time he'd been in Virginia City.

"Hi, handsome," she said, eyes dropping down to the gun in his hand. "Kinda nervous tonight, aren't we?"

Longarm squinted into the shadows. "Alice?"

"I'm flattered that you even remembered."

Longarm holstered his gun. "You shouldn't sneak up on a man that way. Especially a lawman."

She smiled and now he realized that she had been sitting on the front porch swing. Alice had a beautiful smile, and though the light outside the Ore House was poor, she still appeared as lovely as ever. "Custis, you didn't used to be so nervous. Won't you come and join me for a while? It's a lovely evening."

"I'd really like to, but it's been a long, long day. Does your mother still own this hotel?"

"No," Alice said. "She passed away last winter. I own it now."

"I'm sorry about your mother. She was a very gracious lady."

"Yes." Alice sat back down. "I miss her dearly. She liked you very much, Custis. She would talk about you and me long after you returned to Denver. She thought you had made a mistake in not making a respectable woman out of me."

"Maybe I did," he agree with a tired smile as he sat down beside her on the swing. "How have you been?"

"I'm doing fine. Business is nothing like it was when the mines were in full operation and I fear that they never will be the same again. But I like it here and the mansion is completely paid for."

"You'll do fine."

"I know," she said, taking his hand. "But I still haven't found the man of my dreams. I keep waiting for another knight in shining armor to sweep me off my feet."

"Don't give up hope."

"I did find one . . . once," she said quietly. "You were that knight but you rode off alone."

"Alice. Let's not—"

"I'm sorry. You don't like to get too serious, do you? I'd forgotten how you like to keep things simple."

Longarm stood up. "I've seen three dead men today. I'm sorry, but I'm not in the mood for banter and certainly not for a quarrel."

Alice grabbed his hand and pulled him down. "I'm the one that should apologize. Just sit with me for a few minutes and let's talk of pleasant things."

"All right."

"And if we can't think of much pleasant to talk about, we can at least gaze up at the moon and the stars. Can't we?"

Longarm craned his head back to see an almost full moon. "It's a fine night."

"Yes," she said, laying her head on his shoulder and beginning to hum a soft lullaby. "It certainly is. You'll only be staying as long as it takes to find the throat slasher."

"That's right."

"I think he is insane. He has us all frightened. Even the tough, hard-bitten miners out there living on their claims. I hear that he killed two more last night."

"That's right. I saw them coming up the road from Reno. It wasn't pretty."

"Murder never is," Alice said. "Do you have any clues?"

"A few, but they don't amount to much."

"Just be very careful."

"I will." He considered telling her about the death of Marshal Rucker, but rejected the idea, knowing that piece of news could wait until morning. "That's why I came here tonight to sleep."

"You can sleep in my bed. I'll watch over you."

He stroked her hair. "That won't be necessary."

"Probably not, but wouldn't it be nice to have someone taking care of you for a change?"

"Yes, it would." He could not stifle a loud yawn.

"Then it's settled," Alice told him. She helped him to his feet, saying, "You smell pretty bad."

"I haven't had a bath in a while."

"Tomorrow morning you will. Remember how we used to wash each other?"

"Alice," he warned. "Don't remind me of such things tonight."

"Then what about tomorrow night?"

He had to grin. "Tomorrow night will be just fine."

She took his arm and helped him inside, then up the stairs to her big bedroom. Alice undressed, then assisted him to bed. Longarm started to watch her undress but then he fell asleep.

Chapter 15

Longarm awoke at daybreak while Alice was still sleeping. He eased out of her bed, then dressed quietly and left the hotel and walked down to nearby café where he ordered coffee and a good breakfast. By the time he finished, the sun was well up and the street was beginning to fill with wagons and people going to work either in the mines or the various businesses.

As he walked up C Street, Longarm had no particular plan of action in mind but he did want to see if he could locate the medicine wagon as well as find a horse whose hoofprint matched the one he had identified as belonging to the killer. But first, he went to Marshal Rucker's office and examined the papers both in his desk as well as that of Deputy Boone. He was hoping that there might be a note or some evidence as to who could have smothered Rucker. Also, he was not completely convinced that Deputy Boone was innocent of any wrongdoings.

But there was nothing of interest to be found on either desk, so Longarm locked up the office and went searching for answers. First he stopped and made sure that his own horse was doing well and then he checked the other animals being boarded and talked to the owner, a Mr. Pendergast, asking him if he ever remembered seeing a big buckskin with a corrective shoe.

"Can't say as I have," the man replied. "Are you sure that it was a buckskin?"

"No," Longarm admitted. "It could be any light color, I suppose."

"Well, a fella came around yesterday trying to sell me a dun horse. It was a big, stout gelding and it had a corrective shoe on its . . . let's see. Left front foot."

Longarm felt his pulse quicken a beat. "You say it was a dun gelding?"

"Yep. Big fella, too. That horse must weigh twelve hundred pounds and stand sixteen hands. I liked him pretty well, but the man wanted too much money."

"What did the owner look like?"

"He was kinda a runty fella. Maybe five-foot-six and he couldn't have weighed over a hundred and forty pounds."

"Oh," Longarm said, tasting disappointment. "That couldn't be the man that I am after."

"Sorry, then."

Longarm started to turn away, then hesitated. "Look," he said, squatting on his heels. "The horse that I'm searching for had a print that looked like this."

He drew the hoofprint exactly as he'd seen it up on the hill. "Did the dun's foot match this print?"

"Exactly," Pendergast said. "I'd have bought the horse, except that the fella wanted too much money. And I don't like to own horses with problem feet. You know, if the foot goes, the whole horse is worthless."

"That's right," Longarm agreed, staring at the print he'd drawn in the dirt. "Maybe this fella hadn't owned the horse for very long."

"That's sure a possibility. He said he was a horse trader, but I didn't ask him how he came into owning the dun. I would have if we'd started dickering in earnest."

"Had you ever seen this man before?"

Pendergast shook his head. "Nope."

"Describe him in more detail."

"Well, like I said, he was small. He wore high-heeled riding boots. They were pretty fancy and he wanted to show off their tops so he tucked his pants legs into them. I remarked how I'd never seen any prettier boots. They had a red eagle stitched into the leather. Can you imagine what them boots must have cost?"

"Plenty," Longarm said, his interest picking up again. "Did this fella wear a hat?"

"Yep. A tall cowboy hat with an eagle feather in the band. And he had a red bandana tied around his neck and I could tell he had money because he wore the prettiest diamond and ruby ring you ever did see."

Longarm blinked. "Did it have little diamonds encircling that red ruby?"

"Why, how'd you know?"

"Just a lucky guess. Did this fella say he was going to stay in town or was he just passing through?"

"He didn't say. When I told him that I couldn't pay what he was asking for the dun horse, he said he guessed he'd go make the rounds at the other liveries. I told him that Virginia City wasn't a good place to sell a saddle horse. Hay is awful expensive up here, and when someone has to use a horse, they usually rent one."

"I really need to find this man. Is there anything else that you can think of that might help me track him down?"

The livery owner's brow furrowed in thought. "Well, he did say that he had business to do in Gold Hill. He mentioned somebody's first name but I can't recall it."

"Are you sure?"

"Of course I am."

"Did he smoke cigarettes?"

"Not while he was here."

"All right," Longarm said. "I think I'll saddle up that

bay horse I left here and ride down to Gold Hill."

"If you see that man on his horse, you'll see that he sticks out in a crowd. Little bantam rooster all decked out like a cowboy on this great big dun horse. Horse is way too big for the man. You know, a man and horse ought to sort of fit together. A big man like yourself looks stupid on a runty little horse with his stirrups damn near touchin' the ground."

"That's right," Longarm said. "Just show me my saddle, bridle, and I'll get going."

Pendergast scratched his head. "You're a federal marshal, right?"

"That's right."

"Well, why would a man like you have such an ugly horse as that bay?"

"Long story and I haven't got time to explain."

"I understand. You don't think that it was the runty little horse trader that smothered Marshal Rucker, do you?"

"I don't know, but I'd like to ask the man some questions."

Pendergast showed him the saddle and helped him carry his tack out to the corral where the ugly bay was standing. As Longarm saddled the bay, the livery owner said, "That little fella did have a peculiar way about him."

Longarm tightened the cinch asking, "What kind of 'peculiar way' are you talking about?"

"Well, he was armed to the teeth. Wore two guns, one on his right hip and the other in a shoulder holster. And he had a big Bowie knife sheathed on his left hip."

Longarm turned around to see Pendergast standing with his jaw hanging down. "Marshal, you don't think that little fella is the one that has been slashing everyone's throat, do you?"

"I don't know. He might simply have bought the dun horse from someone who *is* the killer. Or, it might not even be the right horse. But what I do know is that the only way I'm going to find out is to track the man down and ask him some hard questions."

"He might have sold the dun to one of the other liveries. If he did, you'd be wasting time looking for that animal down in Gold Hill."

Longarm realized the truth of Pendergast's words. "Well, he said, I don't have time to go to every livery in Virginia City this morning. That would take too long and then I might miss the man if he is only traveling through Gold Hill. So I guess I'll go down there first and just hope he didn't sell that dun yesterday."

"If he's on that horse, he'll stand right out," Pendergast promised. "You sure won't have to worry about missing him in a crowd."

"Thanks," Longarm said as he finished saddling the ugly bay. He mounted the horse and reined it away from the corral.

"You still owe me some board money!"

"I'll be back!" Longarm promised as he pushed the gelding into a trot and headed for nearby Gold Hill.

He had not gone more than a block, however, when he heard Dudley Applewhite shouting his name. Longarm reluctantly reined in the bay and waited for the young marshal to catch up with him.

"Where are you going in such a hurry?" Dudley shouted, fighting for breath because he'd had to run several blocks before Longarm had heard his shouting.

"I got a tip that someone tried to sell a horse that fits the description of the one we are looking for. The man mentioned that he had business in Gold Hill, which is about three miles up the road."

"Why didn't you tell me!" Dudley shouted, still puffing. "I mean, I'm part of this investigation, too, aren't I?"

"Yes, you are," Longarm told him. "And I want you to go to every stable in town and look for a dun horse—not a buckskin—but a dun. If you find the horse, then come down to Gold Hill and look me up."

"Don't it make more sense for me to come along with you right now?"

"No," Longarm said starting off again. "Just do what I ask."

"Damn it!" Dudley shouted. "How come you get to do the exciting things and all I get to do is trudge around looking for a horse!"

"Because I'm in charge," Longarm shouted back over his shoulder.

As he rode toward the Divide, a rise that separated Virginia City from Gold Hill, which was farther down the canyon, Longarm knew that he'd angered his young friend. But it was important to know where that dun horse was located, and there was a fair possibility that its previous owner had already sold it in Virginia City to one of the other stables. In that case, it might mean that the man they were looking for was still up on the Comstock.

Longarm crossed over the Divide and headed down a very steep part of the road into Gold Hill. Virginia City's sister city was just as busy and bawdy as he'd remembered. The only difference was that there were fewer miners digging into the hills on both sides of the steep canyon and two of the big ore stamping mills were closed. But the Gold Hill Hotel and Paddy's Store and the Miner's Rest were still attracting a lot of business. When Longarm passed them he slowed and had a good look around in search of a big dun horse. Not seeing the animal, he rode on down to the next town named Silver City.

He finally got lucky. At the Silver City Saloon, he saw the horse he was searching for. It was tied up to the front hitching rail and Longarm reined his bay in next to it. The bay was as tall as the dun and the two formed an immediate dislike for each other. The bay bit the dun on the neck and got bitten in return.

"Stop it, damn it!" Longarm shouted, jumping between the two cantankerous geldings. But the bay had no intention of quitting the fight. Ears pinned back, it tried to kick the dun and Longarm almost got hit. He had to drag his horse off to another hitching rail and snub it down tight. "You sure are a pain in the butt," he swore at the bay whose pencil-thin neck was arched around as it continued to glare at the much handsomer dun horse.

Longarm went over to that animal and picked up its left front foot. Sure enough, the corrective shoe was the one that he'd been looking for since he'd heard about it down in Reno. Now, it was not entirely impossible that there couldn't be another horse in the county with exactly this kind of shoe, but that was not very likely.

"I think you're the one," he said to the dun as he dropped the animal's hoof and eyed the saloon. "And I hope that your owner is my man."

He made sure that his marshal's badge was hidden and entered the dimly lit saloon. Right away he saw a short, runty fellow wearing a big ten gallon hat. The man was leaning up against the bar, one of his fancy cowboy boots propped up on the brass foot rail.

Longarm eased his pistol up in its holster. He could see that the little man was in his late twenties and decided the man might be a professional gunfighter. As far as Longarm was concerned, it was always far better to overestimate rather than underestimate your potential opponent.

He stepped up to the little man's right side and quietly asked, "Is that your dun horse outside?"

The man twisted around. He had a long but thin face and deepset eyes. He wore a pale mustache and goatee that almost reached the red bandana tied around his neck. He had to crane his head back to look up into Longarm's eyes.

"So what if it is?"

"I hear he is a good horse and that he's for sale."

"Where did you hear that?"

"Up in Virginia City." Longarm smiled. "Is he still for sale?"

The small man stepped back from the bar. "He is."

"Can we look at him outside?" Longarm asked, still smiling and appearing to be relaxed.

"Of course . . . if you have seventy-five dollars cash."

"I do," Longarm said, motioning the man to lead the way outside.

When he did, Longarm waited until they had passed through the swinging saloon doors before he reached down and plucked the little man's gun from his holster. When the fellow made a grab for his shoulder weapon, Longarm slammed him up against the way, yanked it out, and tossed it in the street. He didn't forget the Bowie knife, either.

"What do you mean by this!"

"I'm a United States Deputy Marshal and I have some questions for you, mister."

Two men who had been standing by the little fellow barged outside and looked as if they intended to get involved until Longarm showed them his badge and growled, "Get back inside and mind your own business."

The pair disappeared and Longarm pushed the little fella down on the steps, then towered over him. "What's your name?"

"What is this about!"

"I'll ask the questions." Longarm noticed the diamond and ruby ring on his finger. "You answer them, starting with your real name."

"My name is Bill Nolan."

"Do you have any documents to prove it?"

"In my wallet there are some papers. One of them is a deposit slip from a Reno bank bearing my name. What else do you need?"

Longarm found the wallet. Sure enough, the papers were there with the name Bill Nolan and a postal address in Reno. "Where are you originally from?"

"I've lived in Reno for eight years." The little man drew back his lips. "Anything wrong with *that*?"

"What's your business?"

"I buy and sell livestock. Mostly horses. I also gamble professionally. I do whatever I can to make money, but I do it above board and within the law. Now are you going to—"

"Tell me about that big dun horse."

The little man took a deep breath and fought to control his anger. "I have the distinct impression that you are not interested in buying the animal. So what, exactly, *is* your interest, Deputy Marshal?"

"Just tell me where and how you came about owning that horse." Longarm leaned closer. "And, if you lie to me, I'll know it and I'll arrest you."

"On what charge!"

"Murder."

"You're crazy!"

"Maybe," Longarm told the man. "But you had better believe I'm dead serious."

Their eyes locked. The little man finally looked down at his lap and hissed, "I only bought the gelding yesterday."

"Oh, yeah?"

"Yeah!" Nolan glared up at him, eyes radiating hatred.

"Can you prove it?"

"Hell, yes. I have a bill of sale signed by the previous owner. I'm a professional. I wouldn't buy a horse without a bill of sale."

"Let me see it and, when you reach inside your coat, you'd better not bring out any surprises."

Nolan eased his hand into an inside coat pocket and retrieved a bill of sale. Longarm opened it up and read

155

the few lines that said: FOR THE CONSIDERATION OF FIFTY DOLLARS, I JOHN SMITH, DO SELL A BIG DUN GELDING WITH A FIXED LEFT FRONT FOOT.

The paper was signed with a smudged X written with a soft and blunt pencil. Longarm handed the paper back to the little man. He didn't know if the paper was legitimate or not. This man could easily have written it and added the X for himself, if he were that clever.

Longarm jammed the paper back into his coat pocket. "Tell me all about John Smith . . . or whatever his name really is."

"Not much to tell."

"Do the best that you can or you're headed for a jail cell."

"I have rights. I have a lawyer in Reno and I'm going to see that he sues you for false arrest and detention."

"Fine," Longarm replied. "Tell me about the man that sold you that dun."

"He didn't exactly sell him to me."

"What does that mean?"

"It means I won him playing poker on the night before last."

"If that was the case, why did he sign the bill of sale with his X?"

"Because the horse was in consideration for his fifty dollar bet. And, like I said, I never buy an animal without a bill of sale."

Longarm did not look down at the jeweled ring. "Did you win or buy anything else from the man?"

Nolan sighed. "As a matter of fact I did. I won this ring from him the hour before I won his horse. I got lucky, and he wasn't that smart or good of a poker player."

"Anything else?"

"No. He was mad and I didn't want to take his clothes because they wouldn't have fit."

"He was big?"

"As big as you."

"Describe him in detail."

Nolan filled his lungs and then expelled his breath slowly. "Do you mind if I retrieve my pistols before someone runs over them with a freight wagon?"

"Sit tight and I'll get them," Longarm told the man.

He got the pistols and shoved them behind his gun belt; then he motioned Bill Nolan to climb back up the stairs and take a seat in one of the porch chairs.

"So what did John Smith look like?"

"He was a walking abomination in his early to mid-sixties. A big, very ugly, and coarse man with shaggy white hair and red, watery eyes. His nose had obviously been broken many times in fights, and his face was hatch-marked with scars. He was missing part of his right ear and someone had once cut across his face with a knife, for there was a very deep scar. Oh, and he was missing his left forefinger."

Longarm was surprised and, he had to admit, impressed. For the first time, he began to think that this man was telling the truth or else his mind was extremely nimble.

"I want you to come back up to Virginia City with me."

"No."

"You can do it voluntarily, or you can do it under arrest," Longarm told him. "Which is it to be?"

"When my lawyer gets through with you you'll be the sorriest man in Nevada."

"That might be so," Longarm agreed. "But for now . . . I need you to help me find the man that sold you that horse and then make a positive identification."

"Has this got anything to do with the murders and throat slashings?"

"It does."

"Then I'll cooperate," Nolan decided. "I knew and liked one of the victims."

157

"Thanks. Now let's get on our horses and ride. There is no time to waste."

"I don't think that we have to hurry," Nolan said as they went to their horses.

" "Why is that?"

"The man that sold me this buckskin lives in Virginia City."

Longarm had been about to put his foot into the stirrup, but now he paused. "How do you know that?"

"He told me he did. Said he lived in town."

"Did he say exactly where in town?"

"No, but I had the feeling he worked for someone. From the size and roughness of his hands, I'd say he worked hard when he was sober despite his age and deteriorating physical condition."

"Mount up."

After they mounted and started to ride back over the Divide, Longarm's bay shot his ugly head out and took a big piece of hide off the dun's shoulder. The dun squealed in pain and anger and tried to retaliate but Nolan reined it away. "Jeezus," the small man shouted. "That bay isn't only ugly . . . he's mean!"

Longarm shook his head knowing he could not argue the point.

Chapter 16

Longarm and Bill Nolan left their horses at the livery, but only after warning the owner not to put the two animals in the same pen.

"They don't like each other," Longarm explained.

"That bay don't like any other horses," the man replied. "He's the orneriest and ugliest animal I ever saw. You'd be doing the horse world a favor if you shot him in his big homely head."

"Well, I'm not about to do that," Longarm told the man.

"Your young friend has been here a couple of times today."

"The one with the Boston accent?"

"That's right. He's been looking high and low for a dun with a corrective shoe on his left front foot."

"Well," Longarm mused, "at least he's trying."

Longarm quickly described the man that had sold the dun to Bill Nolan. "Do you know who he is talking about?"

"Sure! A man that big and ugly ain't easy to forget. His name is Ivan Boone."

"Is he related to the one that was Marshal Rucker's deputy?"

"I don't know. I never seen them together, but that's possible. They're both big and ugly."

"Where can I find Ivan?"

"He works for the Comstock Excavation Company. They dig holes in the ground for foundations, sewers, cellars, or anything else you'd want to put in the ground. They'll even dig and muck out old mine shafts that someone new thinks might deserve a second look. It's got to be a tough job because the ground we are standing on is mostly rock. I've seen Ivan with a pick and shovel in his bare hands many a time, and he's a horse when he's sober and feeling right."

"Where can I find the company?"

"Down near the V & T Railroad yard. They got their own yard right close and you can't miss it. Do you think that Ivan is—"

"I don't know," Longarm interrupted. "We just need to talk to him."

"He's a hard, dangerous man just like that former deputy was. I wouldn't want to have to cross either one of them."

"It's my job," Longarm said.

"Marshal," Bill Nolan said. "I've done what you asked. I'd like to take my leave now."

"Just a little longer," Longarm told the man. "Let's walk down to the train yard and find Mr. Ivan Boone. If he's the one that you identify as having lost both that horse and the ring—both of which I have to keep—"

"What!"

"The ring was stolen from one of the murder victims," Longarm explained. "I'm sorry, but you can't keep it."

"Do you know how much this ring is worth!" Nolan cried.

"A lot, but you'll have to turn it over."

The little man swore vehemently to himself. "I sure

160

wish I'd have ridden back to Reno when I had the chance. You'd probably never have found me."

"Oh, yes I would have," Longarm replied. "And maybe you can keep the dun. But the ring will definitely have to be given up, and you might as well do it right now."

"If this don't beat all!" Nolan raged. "I cooperate and for that, I lose a very valuable ring and maybe a horse I won in a card game."

"Hand the ring over," Longarm said, not feeling terribly sympathetic. "I'm sure that the victim will have relatives who will treasure it as a memento of the one they lost."

"Bull! They'll probably sell it." Nolan gave the diamond and ruby ring to Longarm who put it in his pocket. "Any other bad news, Marshal?"

"Nope. Let's go."

"How about giving me my guns and knife back?"

"I will when the time is right," Longarm told him. He was pretty sure that the little dandy was telling the truth, but until he saw and spoke with Ivan Boone, he wasn't taking any chances. Nolan was slick and Longarm wasn't about to underestimate his ability to fake indignation. There was still the possibility that Nolan and Boone were even in cahoots, though that seemed unlikely.

It took them only a few minutes to walk down to the Virginia and Truckee Railroad depot. The V & T, as it was called, made a daily trip down to Carson City, where ore Comstock gold and silver were turned over to the Carson City Mint and equipment and supplies were sent back up to Virginia City. The little railroad also carried a large number of passengers.

"There's the Comstock Excavation Company," Nolan said, pointing.

Longarm had already spotted the little office surrounded by a wire fence topped with barbed wire. They went directly to the office entrance and knocked on the door. A rough-looking man in his fifties opened the door, gave them both a good looking over, and said, "What do you want?"

"We're looking for Ivan Boone."

"He ain't here."

"Where is he?"

"Whose business is it?"

Longarm showed the man his badge. "I need to talk to him."

"Ivan got into more trouble, has he?"

"I don't know. I'll find out when we talk."

"He's old but he's a good worker. If he busted up someone and this is about him payin' the medical bills, then I might see fit to handle the charges. It ain't easy to keep a man at this kind of hard work."

"I'll keep that in mind."

"Was it property . . . or personal damage he did this time?"

"Where is he?" Longarm asked, ignoring the question.

"He's working down at the old Bonanza Mine. It's about a half mile to the north. Some new investors bought it and we're clearing away the rock and debris. The mine goes in about thirty feet and then the shaft drops nearly sixty feet to a lower level. Ivan is repairing the ladder and works so that the new investors can get it back into operation."

"Is he alone?"

"Afraid so. I worked with him earlier this morning. It's tough and dangerous. I couldn't find anyone else that would put up working with Ivan. He's not easy to be around."

"So I've heard," Longarm said. "Give me directions to the Bonanza."

The man did as he was told, and when Longarm and Bill Nolan turned to leave, he said, "Listen. Why won't you tell me what the damages are? If they're reasonable, I'll pay them. Old Ivan won't stand to be arrested. He hates the law, so it'd be better all the way around if you just left him to his work and let me handle this."

"Not a chance," Longarm called over his shoulder on their way out of the yard.

They walked to the Bonanza Mine and as they approached, Longarm could see no sign of Ivan Boone. "He's probably working inside."

"Well, I'm not good about going into caves or mines," Nolan said. "So what are you going to do?"

"I'll leave you out here, if you promise not to run off."

"I won't."

Longarm nodded. "All right then. You wait and I'll go in there and bring Ivan outside. When you see him, all you have to do is nod your head. That will tell me he's the one you got the dun and the ring from."

"There isn't much doubt of it."

"I need a positive identification if I'm going to charge him with multiple murders," Longarm said. "You'll be an important witness when he goes to trial."

"Great," Nolan said sarcastically. "As if I didn't have better things to do with my time. Do you they pay a witness for his time?"

"I don't know," Longarm replied. "It differs from court system to court system. Some do and some can't. A lot of people consider it their civic duty to see that murderers and the like are prosecuted to the fullest extent of the law and taken off the streets."

"How very high-minded," the small man said, voice dripping with derision.

Longarm didn't like Nolan even a little. But the man was cooperating in his own snide, snotty way, and that was what was important.

"Hey, wait for me!"

Longarm looked up and saw Dudley Applewhite standing up on C Street waving.

"Who's that?" Nolan asked.

"My friend."

"He sure can holler loud. Here he comes."

Longarm started to say something, but then he caught a movement out of the corner of his eye. Just a split second of something that had changed at the entrance to the Bonanza. "I'm going in there right now," he said. "When my friend arrives, tell him to wait here with you until I come out of the mine with Ivan Boone."

"Okay."

Longarm drew his sidearm and headed for the dark opening of the mine. He had been in plenty of mines and shafts before and, like Nolan, he was not fond of being underground. In fact, he got damn uncomfortable with all that cold, hard rock surrounding him. But there was no help for this except to go in after his man.

The opening to the Bonanza was about eight feet high and not that wide. Longarm stepped inside and it was as dark as a tomb. But he thought he heard something, and so he raised his gun and shouted, "Ivan Boone. This is Deputy Marshal Custis Long. Come on out. I need to talk to you."

No reply. Dead silence.

"Boone! I said come on out right now!"

The silence deepened.

Longarm swore under his breath. He could wait Boone out, but that might take days if the man had water inside. Also, many of these old mines had other entrances sort of like a prairie dog colony. And while that was unlikely, it was a distinct possibility, and it was one that Longarm knew he could not afford to chance.

"I'm coming in and you'd better step forward!"

Longarm started to reach into his pocket for a match, then thought better of it. If Ivan Boone was a vicious killer, it wouldn't be smart to illuminate himself for the man to target.

"Boone, you hear me!" Longarm shouted, moving into the deepening darkness. "You can't stay in here forever. Come out and talk."

Longarm blundered into a wall, then bounced back and staggered forward. He could feel the hair on the back of his neck standing up on end. Suddenly, he heard a slight rustle of rock underfoot and then his head exploded with light and he felt himself going to his knees. He tried to raise his gun and fire but another blow caught him in the side of the head and his gun went spinning off into the darkness. Longarm rolled instinctively and heard a grunt and a curse. He tried to climb back to his feet and was hit in the chest and knocked over onto his back. Before he could move, Ivan landed on his chest and the next thing Longarm knew he was being hammered by a force that seemed huge and impossibly strong and vicious.

He tried to buck the man off his chest but Ivan sledged him with a blow that left him helpless. Then he felt the killer grab him by the arm and begin to drag his body down the slight decline of the mine tunnel. Longarm realized his life was in terrible danger of being snuffed out. He'd made a huge mistake by not allowing his eyes to adjust to the poor light, which had given Boone an overpowering advantage.

I'm a goner, he thought, trying to muster up some strength but finding it was all gone as lights continued to explode in his skull.

Then Ivan released his arm, knelt by his side, and gave him a mighty shove. Longarm rolled over twice and began to fall. He struck the side of the shaft and lost consciousness, still spinning downward.

Chapter 17

Dudley Applewhite raced up to join Bill Nolan. "Why did he go in there!"

"He thinks that a man named Ivan Boone might be the one that has been killing all those people and slashing their throats."

Dudley bent over and fought for breath. "Damn it, Custis should have waited for me to help!"

"Nothing is stopping you now," the small man said. "But, if I were you, I wouldn't go barging in there for love nor money."

"Why not?"

"If I have to answer that, you're a lot stupider than you look," Nolan retorted. "But do what you want."

Dudley straightened and fought for breath. He drew his new six-gun and started toward the mine opening.

"Custis!" he shouted, peering into the darkness. "Custis, are you all right?"

He couldn't hear a sound. Dudley was still winded and breathing hard. He stepped into the mine and started slowly forward. "Custis!"

No answer.

Dudley swallowed hard. His mouth was dry and he was sweating profusely. The sudden temperature change caused the sweat on his body to chill. The mine was black as midnight, dank, and smelling of sulfur.

"Custis? Please answer me. I can't see a damn thing in here!"

Dudley lit a match. It flared up in his eyes at the very instant that the flat head of a shovel struck him full in the face. Dudley crashed over backward. A man kicked him in the ribs and scooped up his fallen gun. Dudley rolled as shots rang out. Bullets whined off rock, ricocheting down the mine shaft. The man cursed and raced outside.

Barely conscious, Dudley climbed to his knees. He heard gunfire and a cry, then the pounding of feet. Dudley crawled back out to the mouth of the cave. The little man was lying on his back, the toes of his fancy boots pointing to the clear blue sky.

Dudley didn't have to crawl to his side to know the little man was dead.

He pushed himself unsteadily to his knees and staggered over to the entrance of the mine. "Custis!"

There was no answer. Dudley took a step into the mine, but his legs were rubbery and he knew that he could do nothing by himself.

I've got to find help, he thought.

Dudley turned and staggered off in the direction he'd come. He passed the little man with the big hat, which was now soaking in a dark pool of blood. *At least I'm alive.*

He was very unsteady, but he stumbled into a miner's claim and managed to shout a few times. The next thing he knew, he was lying on his back with a crowd of anxious men surrounding him.

"What happened?" one of them asked as he doused his handkerchief with his canteen and wiped Dudley's face.

"A man was shot and my friend is lost and hurt inside the mine."

"Which mine?"

"That one over there," Dudley said, flinging his hand in the direction of the Bonanza.

"Get some rope," the man shouted. "Young fella, maybe you better just lie here and rest. You've taken a hell of a blow against the side of your head."

"Help me over there. Please."

They lifted Dudley to his feet and all went hurrying over to the Bonanza. As they passed the dead man with the big ten gallon hat, the miners shook their heads. "Who did that!"

"I didn't see him."

"Well, I saw Ivan Boone go running off through the sagebrush with a gun in his hand. I'd say that he was the one."

" 'Ivan Boone,' " Dudley muttered, as if he had to imprint the name on his fevered brain.

"He's a bad one," another said. "Let's see if we can find your friend in there."

The miners went into the tunnel and Dudley waited with his heart as well as his head pounding. He heard them shouting and cussing, then distinctly heard someone yell, "He's down at the bottom of the shaft!"

"Let's get him!"

Dudley cradled his head in his hands and rocked back and forth. He sure hoped that Custis was still alive.

Long minutes passed and finally, a man yelled, "I got the rope tied around him. Haul him up, boys!"

Soon, they were dragging Longarm out of the tunnel. Dudley scooted over to his friend's side. Looking up at a miner, it was all he could do to ask, "Is he alive?"

"Must be 'cause he's still breathing. Don't know why, though. He fell a long way."

Dudley felt a wave of relief, but when he looked down into Custis's battered face he wondered if his friend had long to live. How could anyone be that beat up and still be alive? Longarm's clothes had been ripped from his body during the terrible fall. Only his gun holster and boots were intact.

"Let's get him up to see Doc Bartlett. Someone get a wagon down here!"

"Ain't time for a wagon," another miner shouted. "Let's find a couple of planks or a blanket and make a sling. Come on, boys! Put some speed on it!"

Soon, they were all carrying Longarm and helping Dudley back up the hill into town. When they barged into the doctor's office, he took one look at Longarm and Dudley and said, "Lay that man down on the table in the next room. Quick!"

Dudley waited outside with the miners for ten minutes, and when Dr. Bartlett appeared, they all jumped to their feet.

"He's going to live, but it will take some time before he'll be on his feet again," the doctor told him. "He's got some broken ribs and maybe a broken arm. He may also have a concussion and a dislocated shoulder."

"But he will live?" Dudley asked, amazed as the others.

"Yes, I'm sure that he will. He's conscious now and is asking to speak to you."

Dudley hurried past the doctor into the examining room. When he came to Longarm's side he could see that his friend's lips were moving. He had to lean close to hear the words.

"Dudley, are you okay?"

"Yes. I got hit with something in the mine but I'll be all right."

"What about Bill Nolan?"

"Is he the little fella with the big hat and fancy boots?"

"Yeah."

"He was shot twice in the head."

Longarm heaved a deep sigh. "He was the one that could identify Ivan Boone as the fella that sold him the horse."

"The buckskin with the bad foot?"

"Yeah, only it was a dun."

"Is this Ivan the killer and throat slasher?"

Longarm dipped his chin. "He's our man."

"Don't worry. I'll find and capture him."

Longarm reached out and gripped Dudley's wrist. "Wait for me to get back on my feet. Don't go after that man alone."

"But—"

"Listen to me. You're too inexperienced. I'll be up in a day or two."

"I don't think so."

"I will!"

Dudley nodded. "Okay. I'll wait."

Longarm relaxed. "Just be patient. A man that big and ugly can't hide. We'll find him together."

"Sure."

Longarm relaxed and closed his eyes. His every breath sounded labored. Dudley went out of the room and looked at Dr. Bartlett. "Is he really going to be all right?"

"He's a very tough man. He'll make it. Now, let me take a look at your head."

"It's all right."

"I'm the doctor. Let me be the judge of that. Sit down in that chair."

Dudley sank down. His ears were ringing and he felt a bit dizzy, but he figured that would go away soon enough.

"I'm going to put a bandage on your scalp. You've got quite a serious laceration."

"All right."

"You need bed rest for at least twenty-four hours."

"Sure."

"I'm serious!"

"All right."

Dr. Bartlett bandaged his head and gave him some powders to ease his pains. Then, he sent him packing.

"Is the big fella gonna live?" one of the miners outside asked, jumping to his feet along with his friends.

"He is, and I sure do thank you for saving his life down in that shaft."

"Think nothing of it. Sorry that the little fella got plugged."

"Which reminds me," Dudley said. "Someone needs to send the undertaker down there for his body."

"Who'll pay him?" a miner asked. "That's the first thing that the undertaker will ask."

"Tell him that United States Deputy Marshal Dudley Applewhite is in charge of the murder case and will see that he receives just compensation for his services."

"*You're* a marshal?"

Dudley pinned on his badge. "I am. And I'm going after Ivan Boone. Can anyone tell me where to start hunting him?"

"You're going after Ivan Boone? By your lonesome?"

"That's right."

The miners exchanged private glances. Dudley knew that they doubted he was up to the job. No matter. This was his chance to shine. To really put himself on the list of famous lawmen. He would track down and capture Ivan Boone . . . or kill him if necessary.

"Good luck," one of the miners said looking doubtful.

"Thanks."

Dudley polished his badge with the cuff of his coat. Then he headed for the jail, suddenly feeling strong and confident. He'd need to make sure that he had a key to its cell so that, if Ivan Boone did show good sense and surrendered, he'd have a place to incarcerate the infamous killer and throat slasher.

Chapter 18

When Dudley stepped into the marshal's office, he was surprised to see a big man rummaging around in one of the desks. "Who are you?"

"My name is Orvis. I was Rucker's deputy, but I quit when that federal marshal—say, you're wearing a badge."

"That's right," Dudley answered. "I'm Deputy Marshal Dudley Applewhite. Deputy Marshal Custis Long was hurt earlier today."

"Too bad," Orvis said, not sounding very sympathetic.

Dudley frowned and went over to Rucker's desk. He sat down in the chair admiring his badge. "Look, Orvis. I'm about to break a huge murder case and I could use some help."

"Sorry. I'm through with being a lawman. I got a night job as guard for the Ophir Mine. Don't pay much but I don't have to put up with any crap from anybody."

"I understand, but maybe I could hire you personally for just a few hours. I'd make it plenty worth your time."

"Sure," the man said, emptying out a drawer and not sounding very interested.

"I'm serious," Dudley persisted. "I know who has been killing, robbing, and slashing throats around here. If we

175

could capture him, I'm sure that it would be quite a feather in my cap."

Orvis looked up with a drawer in his hands. "*You* know who is behind the killings?"

"Absolutely. And I'll tell you something else. If you were to help me capture or even kill the man—which might be necessary if he doesn't give up voluntarily—it would be quite a feather in *both* our caps."

Orvis forgot about emptying the rest of his drawers. "I might even be appointed Marshal Rucker's replacement, huh?"

"Oh, sure you would! Orvis, I can tell you without a doubt you would be a real hero."

"Hmmm," the big, brutish man mused aloud. "So who is the throat slasher?"

"His name . . . is Ivan Boone."

Orvis almost dropped his drawer. "You don't say!"

"That's right. Do you know the man?"

"As a matter of fact I do."

Dudley could feel his heart starting to pound faster. "Do you know where he lives?"

"Yep."

Dudley clapped his hands together. "Then let's go capture him and make ourselves famous!"

"You got any money to pay me?"

"I—well, I could telegraph for some later, but—"

"Look, Bud. You're asking me to risk my life. Ivan Boone is a bad man. I'd like to know that I'll be paid and I'd like to see the cash in advance."

"But he could be getting away right now!"

"Yeah, he could."

"It will take some time for me to get the money by wire!"

"What do you have of value?"

"Couple of horses, but we'll need them to catch Ivan."

"No we won't. He's hiding just outside of town and

I'm probably the only one that knows where. So, Bud. You sell the horses and bring me the proceeds and we'll go there."

Dudley couldn't believe this man could be so stubborn and greedy. "But—"

Orvis held up his hand. "You're asking me to risk my life."

"But think of how famous we'll become and what it will do for your career!"

"The money," Orvis insisted. "Then we capture bad Ivan."

Dudley cussed under his breath. "All right. I'll be back in less than twenty minutes."

"I want at least a hundred dollars, Bub."

"You'll have it, damn it!"

Dudley took off running for the livery. He was afraid that someone might see or even catch Ivan Boone before he had the opportunity, so he kept his mouth shut and sold his pair of fine horses for much less than they were worth. He even had to sell his saddle to get the total up to one hundred dollars. But it was going to be well worth it. When he had Ivan Boone in jail or laid out on the undertaker's table riddled with bullets—well, his fame would reach all the way to Boston.

"I got the money!" he cried, bursting into the marshal's office and reeling to a chair. He cradled his head in his hands.

"You okay, Bub?"

"I'll be fine. Ivan whacked me with a shovel down in the Bonanza Mine right after he threw Marshal Long down the mine shaft."

"He did all that?"

"Yeah, but now he's about to pay for all his horrible deeds."

"You got that right." Ivan was wearing two pistols in his waistband and one in his holster. He had also confiscated a double-barreled shotgun. He looked extremely formidable.

Dudley gulped. "Orvis, do you really think we'll have to shoot it out with him?"

"I'm sure he'll surrender when he realizes that we're serious and he has no choice but to give up or die."

"I hope you're right." Dudley held out the hundred dollars. "You can count it."

"I trust you, Bub. Now let's go," Orvis rumbled. "Time is wasting."

Dudley headed after the man. He sure was glad that he'd been able to talk this hulking former deputy into helping him. He wouldn't want Orvis to be his enemy for anything.

They marched through town to its outskirts and kept walking. Dudley was feeling woozy and out of breath, but he knew that Orvis wouldn't slow down until they had the throat slasher in their gun sights. Maybe, he thought, Orvis lost one of his friends to the multiple murderer. *I wonder what Orvis's last name is? Forgot to ask, but I can do that later. When the mob of reporters begin to interview then write us up for all the national papers.*

"There it is," Orvis said, coming to an abrupt halt and gazing down at a lonely shack deep in a ravine. "That's where Ivan lives."

"How do we know if he's still there?"

"See that dog sitting in front of his place?"

"Yeah?"

"Ivan loves that dog. He'd never leave him."

"How will we handle this?"

Orvis made a face. "Tell you what. Ivan knows me."

"You've probably had him in your jail a time or two, huh?"

"Oh yeah. I'll go down and catch him off guard then holler when I've got him covered. You can come ahead then."

Dudley shook his head. "I'm sorry, but I insist on being part of the capture. I can handle my end of things."

"You sure?"

"Count on me."

Orvis smiled for the first time and it wasn't pretty. "All right then, Bub. Come along."

"You mean we're just going to *walk* up to that cabin in *broad daylight*?"

"Sure. If we tried to sneak in, Ivan would be suspicious."

"But . . . what if he recognizes me!"

"Pull your hat down low over your eyes. Did he see you in the mine?"

"No."

"Then there's nothing to worry about."

Dudley took a deep breath. Orvis was so big and tough-looking that he was sure the man must know what he was doing. "Let's go then."

They walked right down to the cabin. The dog, a large black-and-white beast with the size and fangs of a Canadian wolf, came charging out at them and Dudley thought sure that it would attack until Orvis shouted, "Hey, Timber. Easy, boy."

The dog skidded to a halt and then, to Dudley's utter amazement, it flopped over on its back, tail thumping the ground. "Geez, Orvis, you sure have a way with ferocious animals!"

"They love me," Orvis said. He cupped his hands to his mouth. "Ivan, we know you're in there. Come on out!"

The door opened and one of the biggest, ugliest men that Dudley had ever encountered stepped outside with a gun in his huge hand.

Dudley raised his pistol. It was shaking in his fist and his voice sounded strange when he shouted, "Drop that gun!"

"Do as he says," Orvis ordered.

Ivan looked from one of them to the other, then dropped the gun. "Orvis, what the hell is—"

"Sorry, Uncle Ivan, but now it's either you . . . or me."

Dudley didn't understand. Ivan didn't either. Suddenly the killer dove for the gun at his feet, and that's when Orvis opened up on him with the shotgun. The blast struck the silver-haired murderer in the chest and knocked him over backward, blood spraying the cabin.

Dudley was horrified. He whirled around just in time to see Orvis swing the shotgun toward him and he reacted on instinct, lifting and firing his pistol. Both weapons exploded at the exact same instant.

Dudley felt himself being slammed backward and then he remembered nothing.

Chapter 19

"Dr. Bartlett! There's been a shoot-out and they're bringing that young federal marshal in with half of his left hand and lower arm nearly blown off by a shotgun blast!"

Both Longarm and the doctor whirled around to see an out-of-breath miner covered with blood. Longarm sat up. "What happened?"

"I don't know! We heard shots and when someone went to investigate, they found the young marshal in bad shape and old Ivan Boone was dead. Then they saw Orvis crawling up through the brush. He unleashed a couple of shots and then vanished in scrub and sage. People who saw him said that he looked to be wounded and in bad shape."

Longarm pushed to his feet and nearly fainted. The doctor grabbed his arm. "Lie back down because you're not going anywhere!"

Longarm started to protest, but then they heard shouts outside and, a moment later, four miners carried Dudley into the office. Someone had used a belt as a tourniquet and Longarm could see that Dudley's forearm, wrist, and hand were mangled beyond recognition.

Longarm eased off the doctor's examining table. "He needs to be here a lot worse than I do."

Dudley was barely conscious. When they laid and then strapped him down, he stared with feverish eyes at the doctor and whispered. "Don't cut it off, Doc. Whatever you do, don't take my arm."

"Lie still. You're going to be all right."

But Longarm wasn't sure. It was a wonder that the kid hadn't bled to death or gone into shock and died. He saw his gun belt and despite the pain, managed to strap it on and make sure that his gun was loaded.

"What are you doing!" Bartlett demanded.

"I'm going to finish this."

"You're insane! You can't even walk to the street."

"Never mind me. Just save the kid," Longarm told the frantic doctor as he threw an arm over a miner's shoulder and said, "I'll need to go find Orvis Boone. Help me."

Another man grabbed him around the ribs, but when Longarm grunted with pain the man eased up. "Sorry. Marshal, you sure ain't in no shape to go out there and try to get Orvis."

"Well," Custis said through clenched teeth. "Unless you want to do it yourself, I have no choice."

The miners exchanged glances, then helped Longarm outside. Custis knew he couldn't walk far. He glanced up and down the crowded street. "We'll use that buggy."

"But it belongs to Mr. Tolman!"

Longarm didn't know who Mr. Tolman was and he didn't really care. "Let's go."

They loaded him in the buggy and headed up the rough dirt road toward old Ivan Boone's isolated cabin and mining claim. When they arrived, Longarm had them help him out. He glanced over at Ivan Boone's blood-spattered body.

"Where did Orvis go?"

"Up that gully," a miner said, pointing. "I stayed here and he ain't gone over the ridge. Orvis might even have bled to death by now."

"If he has, it would be the first lucky break I've had lately," Longarm said, unable to hide his bitterness. "Has someone got a straight-shooting rifle I can borrow?"

"There's a Winchester in Ivan's shack."

"Get it."

Moments later, Longarm was hobbling slowly up the long, brush-choked gully using the butt of the rifle as a crutch. When he glanced back, there was a crowd of curious miners gathered around Ivan Boone's body.

Longarm took a deep breath and continued up the gully. His head was spinning and he felt as if he might pass out, so he knelt and drew in long breaths until he felt a little better.

He can't be more than fifty yards ahead of me. Just hang on a few more minutes and this will all be over. And don't expect a man like that to surrender. He's either dead by now or you're going to have to kill him.

Longarm collapsed behind a large rock and laid his rifle across its rough surface. He aimed it straight up the gully and shouted, "Boone! I know you're wounded. Surrender and I'll promise you a fair trial!"

In response, Orvis Boone stood up and opened fire. Longarm was shocked at how close the man actually was, and, if he hadn't been bent over and unsteady from the bullet that Dudley had put into his side, he might even have won the duel. But Orvis *was* unsteady and he made a big, easy target. Longarm took an extra fraction of a second and shot him. Orvis staggered. Longarm levered another shell into the breech and shot him again, this time in the throat.

Orvis screamed, grabbed his neck, and fell into the brush, thrashing.

Longarm laid his head down across his forearm and breathed deeply. He could hear the huge man flopping around, dying hard, which was exactly the way he had lived.

Damn it, Longarm suddenly realized, now we'll never be sure which one of the Boones was the killer and throat slasher.

Hellfire . . . maybe it was both.

Afterword

Longarm lay on his back in Alice's luxurious upstairs bedroom in the Ore House, a wide smile pasted on his lips as he watched Alice raise and lower herself on his stiff rod. He could feel a tingling pleasure right down to the tips of his toes.

"This is some recovery program you've been putting me through," he panted, looking up at her large bouncing breasts and pretty face. "But I doubt it's what Doc Bartlett had in mind when he said I need vigorous exercise."

"I don't care what Doc had in mind. This is doing more to stimulate your health than any snake oil or medicine."

Longarm couldn't have agreed more. He gripped Alice's hips and thrust his rod harder and deeper into her wet honey pot. "I'm feeling *real* good right now."

"I'm feeling pretty great myself," she giggled, leaning over so that he could lick her hard nipples. "Too bad about your young friend Marshal Applewhite giving up on being a lawman."

"Well, he figured that a one-handed marshal would be pushing his luck. He's fortunate just to be alive, much less still have his arm down to the wrist. Doc Bartlett did a remarkable job."

"Do you think he'll ever find that thief, Marlene, in San Francisco?"

Longarm swallowed hard. "I don't know. I don't care."

Alice threw back her head and moaned with pleasure, telling Longarm she didn't really care either.

Watch for

LONGARM AND THE HORSE THIEF

269th novel in the exciting LONGARM series
from Jove

Coming in April!

Explore the exciting Old West with one of the men who made it wild!